4/99

The Encyclopedia of

CARS

VOLUME TWO – Cadillac to Duesenburg

The Encyclopedia of CARS

VOLUME TWO – Cadillac to Duesenburg

Chelsea House Publishers

Philadelphia

Edited by Chris Horton
Foreword by Karl Ludvigsen

Published in 1998 by
Chelsea House Publishers
1974 Sproul Road, Suite 400
P.O. Box 914
Broomall, PA 19008-0914

Printed in Italy

Library of Congress Cataloging-in-Publication
Encyclopedia of Cars/edited by Chris Horton:
foreword by Karl Ludvigsen.
          p.   cm.
       Includes indexes.
       ISBN 0-7910-4865-9 (vol. 1)
       ISBN 0-7910-4866-7 (vol. 2)
       ISBN 0-7910-4867-5 (vol. 3)
       ISBN 0-7910-4868-3 (vol. 4)
       ISBN 0-7910-4869-1 (vol. 5)
       ISBN 0-7910-4870-5 (vol. 6)
       ISBN 0-7910-4871-3 (vol. 7)
       ISBN 0-7910-4864-0 (set)

1. Automobiles–Encyclopedias.   I. Horton, Chris.
TL9. E5233 1997   97-17890
629.222 03–DC21   CIP

Page 2: Citroën XM 2.5 TD
Page 3: Dodge Avenger ES
Right: Daewoo Nexia GLi 3-door

Contents

Cadillac

U.S.A.
1902 to date

Cadillac began life in 1899 as the Detroit Automobile Company, became the Henry Ford Company briefly in 1901, and was renamed Cadillac after the founder of Detroit in 1902 when it was taken over by Henry Leland, owner of an established machinery and foundry plant supplying the car industry.

Above: 1902 Model A runabout

The first Cadillacs were modest single-cylinder runabouts, but four-cylinder models arrived in 1905, and the 1907 Thirty was a notable success. Meanwhile, Leland had introduced his precision manufacturing methods which allowed parts to be swapped from one car to another. These won Cadillac the R.A.C.'s Dewar Trophy in 1908, and the company won this trophy again in 1913 for its pioneering use of electric lighting, starting and ignition.

Cadillac's success had attracted William C. Durant of General Motors, who added

Above: 1908 Model S runabout

Above: 1909 four-cylinder model

Above: 1911 four-door touring model

the marque to his empire in 1908 to cover the top end of the market. Leland left to found Lincoln in 1917, but advanced engineering remained a Cadillac hallmark. In 1915, the Type 51 introduced the world's first commercially viable V8 engine, as smooth and powerful as the sixes favoured elsewhere but more compact; and 1923 models had an inherently balanced V8 and four-wheel brakes.

1927 was also the year in which Cadillac

Below: 1911 Model 30

Above: 1911 enclosed-body Model 30
Below: 1912 model two-seater runabout

Above: 1913 40/50hp roadster
Below: 1914 Model 30 roadster

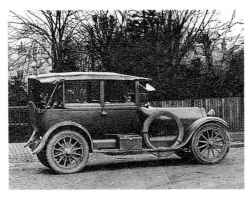

Above: 1916 Model 53 with V8 engine
Right: 1918 Type 57 V8 limousine

was joined by a companion make, the La Salle. Studies made by G.M. had shown that there was a gap in the market for a car in the upper-medium-price range, between Buick and Cadillac, and that the Cadillac division was the better placed to build it. Thus, just as Oakland was joined by Pontiac, Oldsmobile by Viking, and Buick by Marquetta, so La Salle became Cadillac's second make.

It was a La Salle which became the first G.M. car to have styling by Harley Earl, although Cadillac followed close behind. The first La Salle models were essentially lighter and smaller Cadillacs even though the two marques retained their

Left: 1929 Model 341B with Fisher body

Below: By the time this 1926 Model 314 seven-passenger car was built, the V8 engine was an inherently-balanced type and all Cadillacs had four-wheel brakes.

Above: Harley Earl styled the 1929 models

independence of one another; but by 1931 the La Salle was almost identical with the contemporary smaller Cadillac, and shared both its engine and its chassis.

The Depression hit La Salle hard and

Above: 1931 V-16 Phaeton
Below: 1932 V-12 convertible coupé

G.M. planned to drop the marque after 1933, but Harley Earl's attractive proposal for the 1934 models swayed the balance and the La Salle continued. Sales were never enormous, however, and in the late 1930s La Salle and Cadillac grew too close to one another once again. The last La Salle models were built in 1940, after which date the market gap was plugged by the top Buicks and by a revived 'cheap' Cadillac, the Series 61.

The 1930s saw the advent of the

Above: 1932 La Salle Type 345B sedan   *Below: 1933 Cadillac Series 355C*

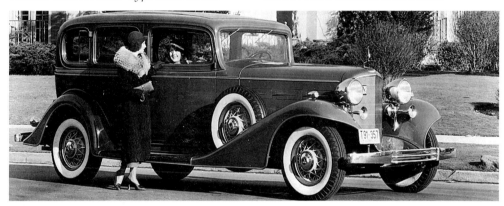

multi-cylinder supercar, and Cadillac was among the pioneers in this field with its fabulous 425-cubic-inch V16 engine, introduced in 1930. This was followed

Left: 1935 La Salle 350 straight-eight
Below: 1937 Series 85 V-12 town car

later the same year by a 368-cubic-inch V12, actually conceived at the same time and designed to use a number of common parts. Although the V16 would always be a loss-leader after 1933 (and was replaced by a cheaper version in 1948), the V12 competed effectively with similar engines from other U.S. manufacturers throughout the 1930s. A wide range of bodies was

available on both chassis, and the styling and appointments of the fashionable Fleetwood bodies did much to enhance Cadillac's reputation as a producer of top-quality cars. Meanwhile, the mainstream models retained V8 engines, and styling remained in the hands of the Harley Earl studios.

Cadillac was kept afloat during the Depression by the sales of cheaper G.M. marques, but Alfred P. Sloan, who had been the Corporation's President and Chief Executive since 1923, recognized that the division could not afford to rest on its laurels indefinitely. There were major changes in 1934 under Cadillac's new General Manager, Nicholas Dreystadt, with new styling and an independent front

Left: 1937 Series 75 'turret-top' sedan
Below: 1949 Series 62 Touring Sedan

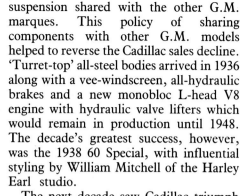

suspension shared with the other G.M. marques. This policy of sharing components with other G.M. models helped to reverse the Cadillac sales decline. 'Turret-top' all-steel bodies arrived in 1936 along with a vee-windscreen, all-hydraulic brakes and a new monobloc L-head V8 engine with hydraulic valve lifters which would remain in production until 1948. The decade's greatest success, however, was the 1938 60 Special, with influential styling by William Mitchell of the Harley Earl studio.

The next decade saw Cadillac triumph over its rival Lincoln and the traditional market leader, Packard, to become the top American car status symbol. The 1941 models introduced rear wheel spats, while 1942 saw fastback styling on the few cars built before Cadillac turned over to war work. The 1946–47 cars were face-lifted 1942 models, but these were followed by significant advances for 1948 and 1949, and it was these which established Cadillac as an industry leader.

For 1948, a long-standing criticism that Cadillac models looked too much like lesser G.M. marques was countered by the introduction of the two-door Sedanet model of kicked-up trailing edges to the rear wings, inspired by the twin tailplane of the Lockheed P-38 fighter aircraft. These began a trend which culminated in the tail fins seen throughout the industry

Below: Like other GM marques, Cadillac contributed to the Motoramas of the 1950s, which showcased prototypes and 'dream cars' such as this 1954 convertible styled by Pininfarina.

in the later 1950s. Then, for 1949, came a new overhead-valve V8 to replace the ageing L-head design. This was a remarkable engine in many ways: light, compact, robust and powerful, it gave all Cadillacs class-leading 100mph (160km/h) performance, and for the next six years the luxury marque was also a leader in the performance field. There were notable successes at Le Mans in 1950 (by Briggs Cunningham) and at the Daytona Beach Speed Trials in 1954.

However, styling was the real Cadillac watchword between 1949 and 1961, and a series of fabulous 'dream cars' displayed at the G.M. Motorama exhibitions previewed production styling features. Concentrating now on the very top of the market, Cadillac dropped its cheaper models in 1951, standardized automatic transmission in 1952, and introduced the expensive, low-volume Eldorado range in 1953.

Above: 1950 Series 62 with overhead-valve V8
Top right: 1956 Eldorado Biarritz Convertible
Centre: 1957 Eldorado Brougham
Right: 1952 Series 62 two-door Sedanet
Far right: Custom-built 1959 Series 62
Below: Destined never to go into production, this 1957 Eldorado Brougham was a Motorama Show Car.

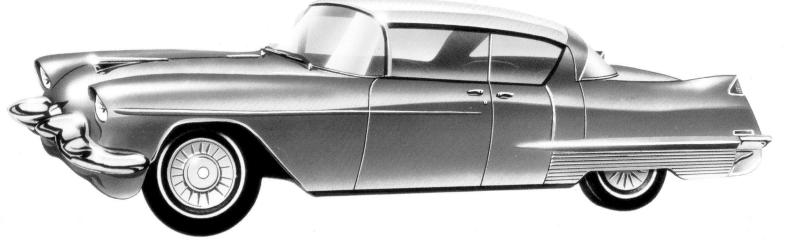

Top: 1959 Fleetwood Sixty Special sedan
Above: 1959 two-door Coupe de Ville
Right: 1959 Series 75 limousine

Long, low, and wide styling now prevailed, and all models sprouted tail fins for 1956, following their introduction on 1955's Eldorado. These grew yearly larger, reaching their zenith in 1959.

Meanwhile, a new chassis design in 1957

had permitted even lower and sleeker lines, and the twin headlamps first seen on that year's top-of-the-range Eldorado Brougham became standard for 1958. Air suspension was also tried on the Eldorado

Brougham models between 1956 and 1960. Central locking and cruise control became available for 1960, in which season the flamboyant styling was toned down.

A new V8 engine, shorter and narrower

Above left: 1960 Eldorado Seville
Above: 1960 Sedan de Ville

than the existing design, made its appearance in 1963, and for 1965 there was a new perimeter-frame chassis which permitted a lower floor level and allowed the engine to be further forward without upsetting the weight distribution, thus giving more length in the passenger cabin. But it was styling and appointments rather than engineering which attracted attention to the Cadillacs of the early 1960s.

The 1964 models, for example,

Above: 1962 Series 62 four-window sedan

Above: 1964 Series 62 Coupé

Below: 1965 Calais hardtop coupé

Below: 1963 Coupe de Ville

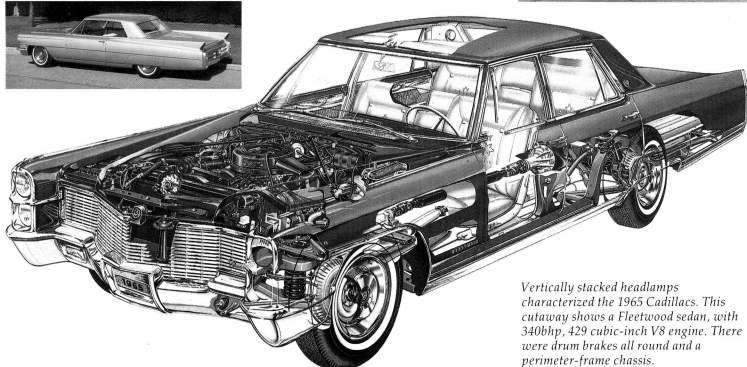

Vertically stacked headlamps characterized the 1965 Cadillacs. This cutaway shows a Fleetwood sedan, with 340bhp, 429 cubic-inch V8 engine. There were drum brakes all round and a perimeter-frame chassis.

Above: 1967 Fleetwood Eldorado

Top: 1965 Fleetwood Eldorado
Above: 1962 Fleetwood Sixty Special

Below: 1974 Fleetwood Eldorado
Bottom: 1974 Coupe de Ville

introduced the option of a padded vinyl roof covering (which was later enthusiastically adopted right across the industry), together with automatic air conditioning, a courtesy-light delay, and the so-called 'Twilight Sentinel', which automatically switched the headlamps on and off to suit the light conditions. The 1965 models also had cornering lights designed to light the way around corners in the dark.

Some of these items were little more than gimmicks; but as Cadillac styling became less flamboyant – tail fins disappeared altogether for 1965 – so advanced engineering resumed its importance as the marque's foremost characteristic. Thus, the 1967 Eldorado had a front-wheel-drive layout derived from the Oldsmobile Toronado, even though other models retained rear-wheel-drive. Engineering was thrust to the fore once again as new safety and exhaust-emission regulations affected the models of the late 1960s.

The crisply sculpted styling of the 1960s

became more rounded for the 1970s, but the biggest changes were caused by the need to meet ever more stringent U.S. Government fuel economy regulations. Cadillacs became smaller, and in the process lost a great deal of their character as large luxury cars; the 1975 Seville was a compact, European-sized saloon which was more than two feet (61cm) shorter than the contemporary De Ville, a traditional-sized Cadillac. Even the top-model Eldorado had been scaled down by 1979. The big V8s meanwhile grew smaller, and in 1978 were joined by a diesel variant, borrowed from Oldsmobile.

The engines of the 1980s continued this economy trend, with a V6 in 1981, petrol V8s which could run on four, six or eight cylinders, and even a 1.8-litre four-cylinder engine in the smallest Cimarron. Although the big limousines continued to dominate their traditional market, it was clear by the mid-1980s that the smaller Cadillacs, based on other G.M. mass-market saloons, were failing to satisfy public perceptions of the marque.

Even the unusually ambitious Allanté model – the two-seat luxury convertible whose body shell is built by Pininfarina in Italy and freighted across the Atlantic in specially-chartered Jumbo Jets – failed to

Below: 1984 1.8-litre Cimarron   *Top: 1978 Seville sedan*   *Above: 1980 Coupe de Ville*

Above: 1989 Brougham

bring the sales or prestige Cadillac had hoped for. But this cumbersome and costly manufacturing arrangement did spotlight Cadillac's keenness to equal the appeal of European imports, especially BMW, Jaguar and Mercedes-Benz.

Above: 1989 Coupe de Ville

Below: Pininfarina styled the 1988 Allanté, a two-door 'personal car' aimed at Mercedes-Benz SL buyers and powered by a 170bhp V8 engine. It was a new type of car for Cadillac.

Top: 1989 Allanté luxury sports model
Centre: 1989 Fleetwood Sixty Special
Above: 1989 Sedan de Ville

As the 1990s approached, Cadillac was faced with a new threat. In addition to the European imports, there were now fine Japanese luxury cars being shipped into the country. Lexus, Honda and Infiniti all offered large luxury cars that competed directly with Cadillac. They were all technologically advanced and highlighted how dated Cadillac's designs really were.

To combat this threat, the company had to buck up its ideas and re-think its designs. By the mid-1990s the Cadillac range was all-new and so were the engines. It was the Northstar V8 that really showed the world that Cadillac could compete technically with the Japanese. It was an all-alloy V8 with two camshafts per cylinder bank and four valves per cylinder. The engine was built to last and was designed to travel 100,000 miles before the first scheduled tune-up. It could even run without its coolant. Should a coolant leak occur, the engine could continue to run safely in limp-home mode by cycling air through deactivated cylinders to cool the engine. Power outputs were impressive too. The top specification Northstar V8

produced 300bhp.

Other technical wizardry appeared in the form of computer-controlled variable-rate dampers, anti-lock braking, traction control, variable-assist power steering and

Above: The 1998 Cadillac DeVille, the saloon version of the Eldorado

Below: The Cadillac DeVille D'Elegance featured more chrome than the standard car

StabiliTrak, Cadillac's unique stability control system.

A new departure for Cadillac was the Catera, a luxury version of the Opel Omega V6. Launched in 1996, the car was the entry-level Cadillac, designed to attract younger buyers, competing with the top import competitors like the Lexus ES300, Mercedes-Benz C-class, and BMW 3-series. It was an important market sector, with the entry-luxury segment making up 40 per cent of the luxury car market.

The Eldorado two-door, and DeVille, its four-door sister, were classic Cadillacs, available with the Northstar V8 and an alarming level of luxury. The Seville, a muscular-looking saloon, was the performance model capable of 150mph.

Cadillac's plans, as the new millenium approached, included expanding abroad with new distribution channels, as well as a new global car. It was estimated that 20 per cent of sales of the new Seville for 1998 would be outside the United States. There were even plans to make a right-hand-drive model. Relatively compact dimensions also increased appeal to foreign markets.

Top left: Cadillac DeVille Concours

Above: 1998 Eldorado

Left: 1997 Cadillac Catera

Below: Eldorado Touring Coupé

Chadwick
U.S.A.
1904–1916

Lee Sherman Chadwick was an engineer who built his first experimental cars while working for a ball-bearing manufacturer in order to demonstrate the company's wares. He then became a designer for the

The following year the Chadwick Engineering Works was formed in Pottstown, Pennsylvania, conveniently close to a major supplier, the Light Foundry Co. By 1908 a larger factory had been opened and Chadwick was employing 90 men. His cars were finished to a very high standard, trimmed with hand-stitched leather and hickory. Chadwicks were also very fast, with an early lightweight version being timed at over 100mph (160km/h). They are widely

financial trouble. When the Light Foundry Co. refused to supply him he considered setting up his own foundry, but this proved to be a totally uneconomic proposition. The following year this innovative perfectionist left not only his company, but the motor industry as well, for employment with the Perfection Stove Co. Production of his cars went on for another four years, however, and finally ceased in 1916, with a total of only approximately 265 cars ever built.

Searchmont Motor Co., where he was backed in plans for a four-cylinder car. When the backers withdrew and Searchmont went bankrupt in 1903, Chadwick bought the necessary parts and set up to build the cars himself.

The following year he founded the Fairmont Engineering Works to build Chadwicks and repair other makes. By 1906 he had produced around 40 cars and introduced an enormous 11.2-litre-engined vehicle.

considered to be the first high-performance U.S.-manufactured car.

Another first for Chadwick was scored by his competition vehicles, which began hill-climbing in 1908 and later went on to racing. In the Vanderbilt Cup and the Savannah Grand Prize of that year, Chadwicks were fitted with the earliest-recorded superchargers on a petrol engine, although this device was never offered on the company's road-going vehicles.

By 1910, however, Chadwick was in

Above: The enormous 11.2-litre Great Chadwick Six. The six-cylinder engine, called the Type 19, featured an overhead valve arrangement and in a stripped-out car was capable of speeds in excess of 160km/h (100mph).

Chenard-Walcker

France
1901–1946

Ernest Chenard started making bicycles at Asnières, Seine, in 1883, before going into partnership with Henri Walcker in 1898 to make tricycles. Their first venture into car manufacture was an 1160cc T-head twin-cylinder machine which featured coil ignition and a double-back-axle arrangement. Progress was rapid, and by 1906 they were making over 400 cars a year, had become involved with marine engines, and were in a position to go public. This tied in with a move to larger premises at Gennevilliers, Seine, where the company remained until its demise.

Although Chenard-Walcker ventured into light trucks and taxis, the company concentrated mainly on medium-sized, reasonably priced passenger cars. These ranged from a 942cc single-cylinder voiturette introduced in 1910, through a mid-range three-litre model to 6.3-litre straight-fours of 1911. Walcker died in 1910, by which time production had risen to 1,200 cars a year. By the outbreak of World War I annual production stood at 1,500 cars, and included a 4.5-litre six-cylinder model.

After the war, the three-litre model was revived, and some commercials were made using the same engine. These took the form of road tractors, which came to be made under licence by Beardmore in Britain and Minerva in Belgium. By 1931 these vehicles had grown to 250bhp monsters powered by two 7.5-litre Panhard engines.

Chenard himself died in 1922, and his son Lucien carried on the business, supported by the Donnay family and his brother-in-law Georges Stein. A new car designed by Henri Toutée appeared that year, a three-litre single-overhead camshaft straight-four with Hallot servo brakes which acted on the front wheels and the transmission. One such won the very first Le Mans 24-Hour race, and the works entered a four-litre straight-eight. The company also made quite successful 1.5-litre cars with all-enveloping 'tank' bodies.

These were the halcyon days for Chenard-Walcker, who had by now become the fourth-largest manufacturer in France, producing 100 cars a day. It had acquired the firm of Sénéchal, and continued to produce this company's small sports cars. It also made AEM electric vans, and in 1927 entered into a consortium with Delahaye.

In 1933 came the front-wheel-drive models designed by Jean Grégoire. The 2.4-litre model featured independent front suspension and a Cotal gearbox, and some 1,300 cars of two and 2.4 litres were sold.

Above: 1923 three-litre Le Mans
Below: Chenard-Walcker Aigle-8, c. 1936

A 3.5-litre V8 was tried but, by 1936, this diversification was proving a strain and the company was in financial problems.

Coachbuilders Chausson, who had been supplying saloon bodies to Chenard-Walcker and Matford, gained financial control in 1936. Engines now came from Citroën and Matford in the shape of a 1911cc straight-four and a 3622cc V8. The Chenard-Walcker Aigle-8 convertibles had the very attractive Labourdette *Vutotal* ('see everything') pillarless windscreens, and although car production more or less ceased in 1939 with the outbreak of World War II, a few were assembled in 1946.

Chenard-Walcker continued to build light forward-control vans between 1947 and 1951, when it was finally taken over by Peugeot; the van itself survived as a Peugeot until 1965.

Chevrolet
U.S.A.
1911 to date

Louis Chevrolet, from whom the marque name was taken, was a successful racing driver of Swiss descent. He was born in La Chaux de Fonds in 1878, soon moving to Beaune, France, with his family. From there he spent time in Paris, working for Mors, before deciding to head for Canada with his brothers Arthur and Gaston. New York offered new opportunities for Louis, where he worked for car and later truck manufacturer William Walter, and also for the importers of De Dion-Bouton cars.

He then spent varying amounts of time with different manufacturers, becoming well known in competition, and building himself a racer based on a Buick. It was this which brought him to the notice of William Durant, founder of General Motors and former Flint buggy manufacturer. Arthur Chevrolet became chauffeur to Durant, who had, by this time, lost his control over General Motors.

Louis Chevrolet and Durant then got together on the design of a new French-style car, called the Chevrolet in order to cash in on both Louis's and Arthur's racing fame. By 1911 the Classic Six went into production in premises at 3939 Grand River Avenue, Detroit. On 3 November that year the Chevrolet Motor Co. was incorporated, leasing better workshops at 1145 West Grand Boulevard. By 1912 production of the Classic Six had reached 2,999 units.

Chevrolet production moved to Durant's Little Motor Co. in Flint, while the Mason Motor Co., also under Durant's control, supplied engines. The firms merged into Chevrolet in 1913, moving to the Flint Wagon Works and building the Little Runabout as the Little Four. In 1913 Chevrolet launched the four-cylinder Baby Grand Tourer, together with its single-seat version, the Royal Mail. The Baby Grand was the first car to carry the distinctive blue-and-white Chevrolet badge, said to have come from a wallpaper design Durant once saw in a French hotel.

Above: 1914 Baby Grand

In 1913 Louis Chevrolet left to go into partnership with V. R. Hefler and J. Boyer, starting such firms as the Chevrolet Brothers Manufacturing Co. and the Chevrolet Aircraft Corporation. His endeavours failed in the Depression, however, and he died in obscurity in 1941, having worked briefly for Chevrolet during the 1930s.

By 1914 the company bearing his name had purchased the Maxwell Motor Co. plant in Tarrytown, New York, for assembly, and some 5,005 cars were built.

Above: 1917 Type 490

The following year the 490 model was launched, so called because of its $490 price, with Chevrolet going for the economy market. By 1916 production had reach 70,701 and the year after that the first closed-body cars were offered. Commercial vehicles began in 1918, with the Light Delivery and the Ton Truck.

In 1919 Chevrolet became a Division of Durant's old company, General Motors, production by this time running at 149,904, but the post-war economic depression caused losses of U.S. $5 million in 1921 and the company only narrowly escaped closure. G.M. president, Pierre S. du Pont, called in industrial engineers to

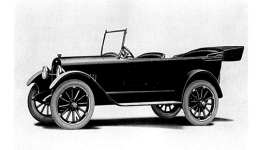

Above: 1919 FB-50 touring car

Above: 1912 Classic Six

Above: 1914 tourer

Above: 1922 Type 490 four-door sedan

assess Chevrolet, who told him that the firm could not hope to compete in the field which it was aiming for. Du Pont's assistant, Alfred P. Sloan, took the statement as a challenge and set out to prove them wrong. In 1922 William S. Knudsen was appointed head of the Chevrolet Division, taking over from Karl W. Zimmershield. Five years later Chevrolet was the largest car manufacturer in the world.

Above: 1923 Superior Series B sedan

Right: 1923 roadster

Below: The 1923 'Copper-cooled' Superior model cost $525 and had an air-cooled engine on a standard chassis. It gave so many problems that all except one car were recalled to the factory.

It was not all easy. In 1923 a successor for the 490, the air-cooled Superior, was such a disaster that it was recalled to the factory. The previous year, however, production had run at 243,479 and Chevrolet had expanded with new plants in Janesville, Buffalo and Norwood, and a pressed-metal plant in Flint was started.

By 1927 Chevrolet had introduced the closed-cab utility vehicle, made 1,001,880

Above: 1928 coupé

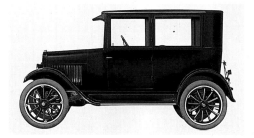

Above: 1924 Superior Series F coach
Below: 1925 Superior Series K coach

vehicles and gained first place in the industry. By the following year it had begun laying plans to adopt a new six-cylinder engine – 'Six for the price of Four' – having survived until then on the four-cylinder overhead-valve unit. It was launched in 1929 and production peaked at 1,328,605. The Depression was weathered without too many problems, with Chevrolet staying the most popular car in America into the 1930s.

Below: 1930 Universal Series AD coach

Below: 1930 Universal sport roadster

Above: 1926 Superior Series V Landau sedan
Below: 1928 National Series AB cabriolet

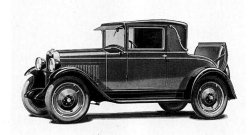

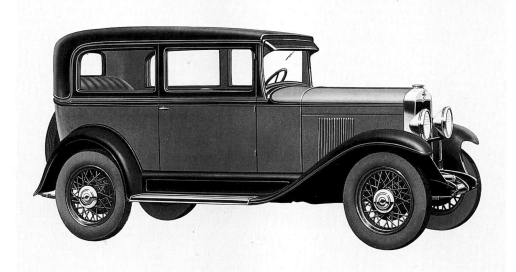

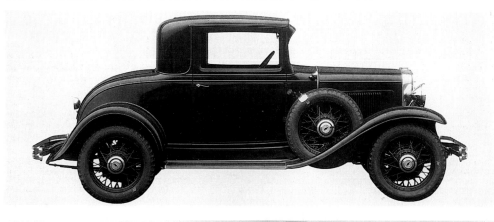

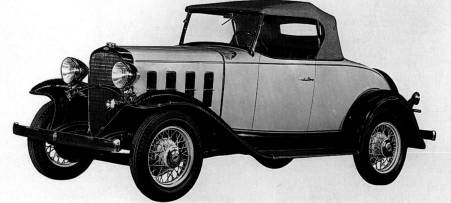

Above: 1933 Eagle Sport Coupé
Right: 1939 wooden-bodied station wagon

Left: 1931 Independence coupé
Above: 1934 Master two-door Town Sedan
Below: 1935 Master De Luxe coach

Above left: 1932 Confederate roadster
Above: 1936 Master De Luxe sedan
Below: 1937 Master De Luxe coach

By 1933 Knudsen had become G.M. executive vice-president and M. E. Coyle became General Manager of Chevrolet. Synchromesh transmission, all-steel body-work (known as the 'turret top') and independent front suspension had all been adopted by 1935, with hydraulic brakes arriving a year later. The ten millionth car was produced in 1935, and the 15 millionth four years after that, when the station wagon joined the Chevrolet range.

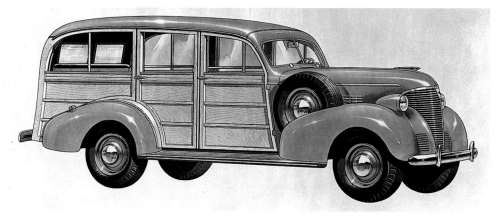

Above: 1941 Special De Luxe Series AH

A phenomenal 1.4 million sales were recorded in 1941, before the company's factories were turned over to war work. That year Juan Manuel Fangio had his first big win in an Argentinian endurance race, driving a Chevrolet coupé.

Above: 1942 Fleetline Aero Sedan

In 1946 Nicholas Dreystadt, formerly of Cadillac, took over briefly from Coyle, but died two years later to be replaced by W. F. Armstrong, a vice-president of

Below: 1947 Fleetmaster station wagon

G.M., and General Managership passed to T.H. Keating. Keating succeeded Armstrong in 1949. The Chevrolets of that year were given completely new styling, and the Bel Air hard-top was introduced in 1950, when Powerglide fully automatic transmission became available even on the cheaper models. Three years later the extraordinary Corvette was launched.

Above: 1949 Styleline De Luxe sedan

Below: 1954 Corvette sports roadster

Above: 1952 Styleline De Luxe convertible

Above: 1955 Bel Air four-door sedan

Above: 1956 Bel Air convertible

Although often credited as the work of Russian engineer Zora Arkus Duntov, the Corvette, designed by Harley J. Earl, was already being constructed when Duntov joined G.M. The car was underpowered to begin with and not noted for stable handling, but Duntov worked to improve the suspension, and the use of a V8 power unit and manual gearbox saw the car take off as a rival for the Thunderbird introduced by Ford in 1955.

Right: 1957 'Two Ten' Sport Sedan
Below: 1958 Delray Utility Sedan
Below right: 1957 Impala Sport Coupé

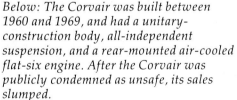

Below: The Corvair was built between 1960 and 1969, and had a unitary-construction body, all-independent suspension, and a rear-mounted air-cooled flat-six engine. After the Corvair was publicly condemned as unsafe, its sales slumped.

Above: 1959 Impala Sport sedan hardtop
Right: 1961 Nomad station wagon

The compact Corvair went on sale in 1959, as did the first of the Impala range, but the former was too unusual for a conservative market to sell well, although it was not dropped until 1969. In 1962

Right: 1961 Corvette

Above: 1961 Corvair 700 coupé

Above: 1962 Impala hardtop sedan

The 1964 Corvette Sting Ray lost the previous year's split rear window but was otherwise little changed. With fuel injection, the Corvette's 5.7-litre V8 engine developed 395bhp.

The Camaro Z-28 was a four-seater sports coupé with a 4948cc V8 engine giving 290bhp. It featured unitary construction, coil-spring-and-wishbone independent front suspension, and semi-elliptic leaf-spring rear suspension.

Above: 1963 Chevy II compact sedan
Below: Some of the 1964 Chevrolet range

Above: 1963 Impala Sport Sedan

came the Chevy II, to bridge the gap between the Corvair and the larger Impala, Biscayne, and Bel Air models. The slightly bigger Chevelle model followed in 1964, together with the Corvette Sting Ray, and the model range was then priced from U.S. $2,028 for the simple 90bhp four-cylinder Chevy II, to U.S. $3,347 for the Caprice Custom station wagon.

The Camaro sports coupé was introduced in 1967, tapping into the booming muscle-car market. It was a late challenge to the Ford Mustang, but more than two decades later the Camaro name – and the classic front-engine, rear-wheel-drive concept – was still exciting driving enthusiasts. Memorably, the Camaro IROC-Z of 1989 adopted the 350-cubic inch (5.7-litre) V-8 of the L98-engined Corvette, its outputs of 240bhp and 345lb-ft of torque allowing a top speed close to 240km/h (150mph).

By the 1970s Chevrolet engines were being used by a variety of other manufacturers in their products. The largest eight-cylinder Opels were Chevrolet-powered, as were the smaller six-cylinder Oldsmobiles. The new version of the 8/10 Cord also used a Chevrolet engine, as did the limited-production Gordon-Keeble and the US–Italian Iso and Bizzarini, as well as Canadian-built products such as Pontiac, Acadian, and the last of the Studebakers.

In the early 1970s Chevrolet bought into the Japanese Isuzu company, beginning to integrate some of that company's models

Above: 1972 Camaro Z-28
Below: 1974 Vega hatchback coupé

Below: 1974 Monte Carlo Landau coupé
Bottom: 1987 Camaro Z-28

into its own range. The fuel crisis caused it hastily to scale down the size of its cars and sales were down, too. The sub-compact Vega was offered in 1971, and two years later the range included the Chevy II, Nova, Monte Carlo, Bel Air, Camaro, Corvette, Caprice luxury model and the Blazer and Suburban station wagon/utility vehicles. Chevrolet brought out what it described as a 'world car' in 1976 in the form of the compact Chevette.

By 1980 the front-wheel-drive Citation was launched, with a transverse engine, and Oldsmobile diesel units were in use in larger V8-engined models. Four years later the introduction of the Cavalier brought great success to the company. In the mid-1980s the company began using its Japanese contacts, offering Isuzu and Suzuki models under different names, and collaborating with Toyota on the 1984 Nova model.

Chevrolet's production of cars and utility vehicles is still among the largest in the world, although it lost pole position in 1980. The company's most interesting current offering is the amazing six-speed Corvette ZR-1.

Top: 1987 Camaro LT
Above: 1989 Caprice Classic sedan
Below: 1989 Beretta GT coupé

Above: 1989 Corsica hatchback

Below: 1989 Camaro IROC-Z

Left: 1989 Celebrity Eurosport sedan

Below: the 1989 Corvette ZR-1 had a 380bhp V8 engine developed in conjunction with Lotus. There was a six-speed gearbox and limited-slip differential. Zero to 96km/h (0-60mph) was claimed to take just over 4 seconds.

By the early 1990s G.M.'s market share had fallen from its peak of 46 per cent in the late seventies to 35 per cent, despite a large increase in the number of staff.

Whereas other companies had more successfully changed with the times, Chevrolet, G.M.'s largest division was starting to look a little old and inefficient. The firm took around a third more man hours to build a car than its Big 3 rivals and losses within G.M. of around $800 million a month were enough to curb spending on new models.

In 1992 Chevrolet had 38 different cars and 80 different truck models. The way ahead was clear; Chevy would have to cut the number of models, so that's just what it did. Management planned to cut 20 per cent by the turn of the century and to reduce the number of different vehicle platforms from 21 to just seven in order to spread out engineering costs and increase the number of common components. This helped to stem the huge losses that the company was experiencing and started to turn the tide of Chevrolet's fortune.

In 1995, G.M. finally abandoned production of its ageing 'land yachts', the full-sized, rear-drive leviathans like Chevrolet's bulbous Caprice. The Caprice plant was switched to truck production, to cash in on the truck's rise in popularity by the mid-1990s. At the same time, the company was undergoing radical changes to its working practices, with Japanese-style

Above: 1998 Chevrolet Blazer four-door LT

management structures, in an attempt to increase efficiency.

By 1997, G.M. had launched more new models than it had done in years and was showing signs of returning to the form of the great company that it had been. One new model that was particularly welcome was the sixth generation Corvette, a high-tech marvel that was easily capable of taking on some of the world's greatest sports cars. Unlike previous Corvettes, it was rumoured that this model would also go to Europe.

Below: Chevrolet Monte Carlo Z34 coupé

Below: Cavalier LS convertible

Above: 1997 Chevrolet Geo Prizm

Above: Camaro Z28 Brickyard 400 pace car

Above: The 1997 Chevrolet Corvette coupé is shown with its ancestors, the previous four styles of Corvette sports cars

Above: Chevrolet S-series pick-up

Above: Corvette convertible

Above: The Tracker was rebadged Suzuki Vitara

Above: Chevrolet Geo Metro LSI

Above: 1997 Lumina Sedan

Above: Regular wheelbase Venture

Chrysler
U.S.A.
1923 to date

In November 1921 Walter P. Chrysler took control of the Maxwell Motor Corporation, outbidding Willys, White, Studebaker and Durant to do so. He became president of the firm and continued producing Maxwell-badged cars for the next four years.

In 1923, however, Chrysler recruited three former Studebaker designers, Owen Skelton, Fred Zeder and Carl Breer to work on a model to be launched under his own name. This appeared the following year as the Chrysler 70, and was produced in Detroit, at the former Chalmers factory. There were 4,000 dealer outlets for the new car, which achieved sales of over 30,000 in that first year. Also in 1925 the Maxwell name disappeared.

Below: The 1926 B-series was offered with a variety of bodies; this is a five-passenger brougham. All the B-series cars had L-head six-cylinder engines and four-wheel hydraulic brakes.

The Chrysler Corporation was formed in June of that year, with capital of U.S. $400 million and seven plants in three different states and Canada.

There were four models offered in the 1926 range, including the sophisticated Chrysler 60, and the first Imperial,

destined to become a separate marque from 1954, which used bodies by various coachbuilders, including Fisher and LeBaron.

In 1927 responsibility for manufacturing was taken over by former General Motors man, K. T. Keller, who went on to become president in 1935. The following year the De Soto line was offered to compete with Pontiac, Oldsmobile and the less-expensive Nashes. To rival the cheap

Left: 1925 Series B-70 tourer

Above: 1926 Imperial E-80

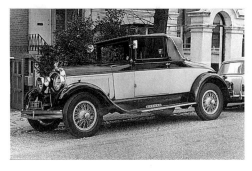

Above: 1928 72 cabriolet
Below: 1927 Chrysler 62

Above: 1926 Chrysler 60

Above: 1929 Roadster

Below: 1930 Model 70 Sportsman's Coupé

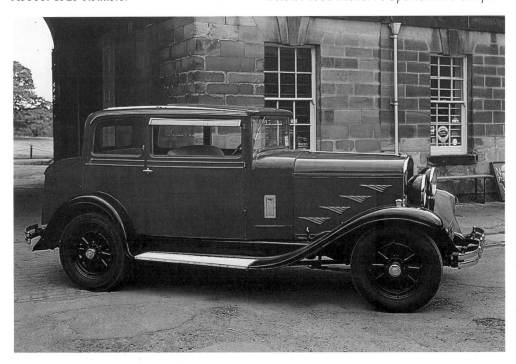

Ford and Chevrolet cars the Plymouth marque appeared the same year. The acquisition of Dodge for U.S. $175 million in 1928 filled the slot just above De Soto's price range, also providing Chrysler with a truck manufacturer, and moved the firm up to third place in the American sales league. Factory space increased five-fold.

Fred L. Rockelman took control of the company from 1930 and the first straight-eight-engined cars were launched the year after. The company survived the Depression only showing a loss in 1932. Chrysler was noted for experimentation and technical development, introducing power brakes, automatic clutches and a free spare wheel in 1932. A new method of rubber mounting engines, called Floating Power, was brought in during this time, and was soon adopted by Citroën. The following year saw the arrival of synchromesh transmission.

In 1928 Chrysler had begun development of a revolutionary new car of streamlined unitary construction which

Above: 1935 Airflow C-1

feature in 1949 was ignition-key starting and two years later came the innovative overhead-valve V8, designed by Chief Engineer Rob Roger, James Zeder, and Owen Skelton, which was followed by Power Flight automatic transmission in 1953. The new engine finally completely replaced the old six-cylinder sidevalve unit in 1955, and was used by a variety of other manufacturers, including Allard, Cunningham, and Jensen in England.

In the mid-1950s Chrysler began experimenting with gas-turbine-powered cars, which boosted its image. Earlier, Exner had helped increase Chrysler's prestige with his range of dream-car designs, actually built by Ghia under the Dual-Ghia name. In 1955 came the new styling, which brought the appearance of the cars up to their interior and build quality.

By 1958 De Soto's sales had slumped so badly that the marque was discontinued two years later. That year Plymouth launched the Valiant compact range, sold under the Chrysler name abroad. In 1965 Virgil Boyd took over as president and Elwood P. Engel was in charge of styling. The V8 Barracuda, a successful model based on the Valiant, was offered that year.

Meanwhile Chrysler had been expanding its interests overseas, taking control of Simca in 1963, and partly purchasing the British Rootes group to form Chrysler United Kingdom Ltd. by 1970. That year the company also gained a 15 per cent holding in Mitsubishi (since reduced to release cash), its later compacts showing

was finally launched in 1934, with the company's new automatic overdrive. The Airflow proved too futuristic for the motoring public and was a commercial disaster, although it was continued for appearances' sake until 1937. Chrysler hurriedly rushed out the less-extravagant Airstream in 1935 to try and salvage sales. This failure caused the company's styling policy to become over-cautious until Virgil Exner's Flite Sweep bodywork of the mid-1950s. Further technical improvements appeared in 1937 – hypoid rear axles and independent front suspension – and in 1939 came a steering-column gear change and optional fluid drive or torque converter.

In 1940 Walter Chrysler died and Keller took over as Chief Executive. Two years later the company went over to war production, making a variety of military equipment, including aircraft fuselages and tanks. Chrysler is still a major tank manufacturer.

Civilian production resumed in 1946 when Town and Country wooden exterior trim appeared on Chrysler models. A new

Below: The 1949 New Yorker had an eight-cylinder engine of 135bhp and could be ordered with Prestomatic semi-automatic transmission. The 1949 models were very conservative in appearance, but had distinctive tail lights.

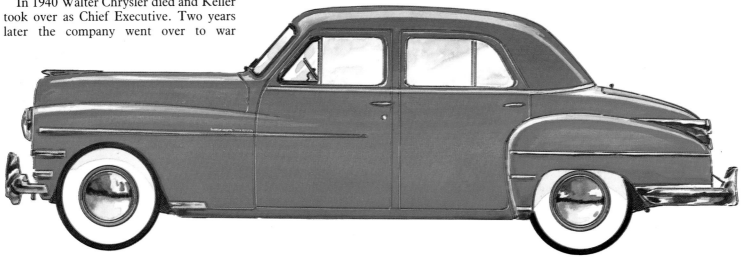

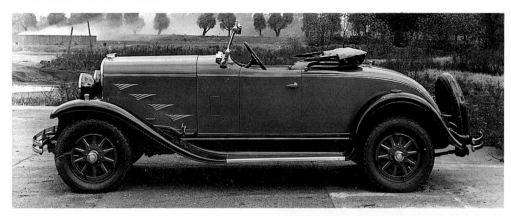

Left: 1930 Series 70 roadster

Above: 1931 CD Eight convertible coupé

Above: 1946 C-38W Windsor Traveler sedan
Right: 1955 C300 coupé

Above: 1975 Chrysler (UK) Alpine S

Left: 1974 New Yorker four-door hardtop

Above: 1976 Chrysler (UK) Avenger Super
Left: 1975 Chrysler (UK) Hunter De Luxe

both French and Japanese influences. The company also had interests in the Barreiros truck company in Spain.

These acquisitions were rationalized during the oil crisis of the early 1970s, and the Rootes-based group only narrowly escaped collapse. South African and South American interests were also affected. E. A. Cafiero became president in the mid-1970s, followed by former Ford chairman Lee A. Iacocca. Chrysler's fortunes wavered between small profits and hefty losses, and at one time it had U.S. $1,000 million debts with 115 different banks. The Imperial line was axed in 1975 and towards the end of that decade four-cylinder cars began to gain importance.

Above: 1977 Chrysler (UK) Sunbeam S

Below: The 1970 Chrysler 180 was actually a Rootes design, but was built in France at the Simca factory which Chrysler owned. Its 100bhp four-cylinder engine of 1812cc drove through a four-speed gearbox.

Top left: 1990 Eagle Talon sports coupé
Above left: Le Baron Turbo GTC
Top: 1990 TC sports coupé
Above: 1990 New Yorker luxury sedan

Above: 1990 Eagle Premier ES sedan
Right: 1990 Le Baron sedan

Below: 1990 Eagle Premier ES Limited

Left: 1990 Eagle Premier LX sedan
Below: 1990 Eagle Summit ES sedan
*Bottom: 1990 Eagle Summit LX sports
sedan*

Mitsubishi engines were increasingly used in the early 1980s, when the respected LeBaron name was revived. By 1982 the company was back in profit, retaining interests in Japan and Peugeot in France. In 1986 came the Chrysler-Maserati collaboration on an image-building convertible the 'T.C. by Maserati', but this relationship was always fraught. In the late 1980s Chrysler acquired American Motors, including Jeep, and also bought Lamborghini, which led to a V12 Formula One engine, and to Chrysler partially severing its ties with Maserati. After the AMC takeover in 1987, Chrysler launched the Eagle marque in December of that year.

Top: 1980 Jeep Cherokee Chief
Centre left: 1990 Jeep Wrangler Laredo
Centre right: 1980 Jeep CJ-7 Laredo

Left: 1990 Jeep Wrangler S
Above: 1990 Jeep Wrangler Islander

Top: 1990 Jeep Wagoneer Limited
Above: 1990 Jeep Grand Wagoneer
Top right: 1989 Conquest TS1
Right: 1990 Chrysler TC by Maserati

Below: The 1986 Chrysler-Maserati
convertible was the result of Chrysler's
collaboration with the famous Italian
maker, but the relationship was not wholly
successful. The Chrysler 2.2-litre engine
was tuned by Maserati.

By the late 1980s, Chrysler was lagging behind the other members of America's Big Three and looked set to continue on a downward slide. However, clever management and design rationalization soon saw the company on the route to recovery.

While many of Chrysler's cars had been Mitsubishi-based during the 1980s, the 1990s saw the company starting to push its own products. The biggest step forward was the development of the L/H range of cars, which some wags in the industry suggested stood for 'Last Hope'. To cigar-smoking Chrysler President Bob Lutz, they meant 'Latest Hit', and he was right.

The new car's cab forward design soon proved popular with buyers, improving the company's sales and image in the process.

The L/H cars weren't just good-looking though; much thought had gone into their design and construction. By economizing without sacrificing quality, Chrysler were able to make more profit per car sold than

either Ford or General Motors.

The success of the L/H cars led to the Neon compact car. The Big Three had by this time largely abandoned building their own small cars, so it was unusual for Chrysler to consider re-entering the market. Building on the management techniques that had brought the company the L/H cars, Chrysler managed to take the Neon from concept car to production vehicle in only 31 months and the project required only half the amount of engineers usually assigned to

Top: The Jeep Cherokee was updated under the skin in 1996 but was outwardly almost exactly the same

Left: 1997 Chrysler Neon

Below: The Chrysler World HQ and technology centre in Detroit

such a project. The cost, too, of $1.3 billion, was a fraction of what is normally spent. Ford's Mondeo project, for example, cost around $6 billion.

While Chrysler's factories didn't even rate in the top 10 most efficient car plants in North America, it was still able to make more profit per car.

The Jeep Wrangler and Cherokee 4x4s continued to sell well in an atmosphere where truck sales were growing rapidly, and had gathered a cult following. The Grand Cherokee, launched in 1992, soon attracted the same kind of following.

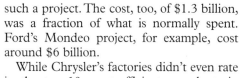

Above: Chrysler Sebring Convertible   *Right: 1998 Jeep Grand Cherokee*

Above: Chrysler Town and Country

Right: 1998 Sebring Coupé

Below right: Chrysler Concorde

Below:: 1996 Jeep Wrangler

42

Cisitalia

Italy
1946–1965

Piero Dusio, founder of Cisitalia, was a professional footballer forced to retire early because of injury. He went successfully into sales for a large textile firm, affording not only to buy his own competition cars, but also to set up Scuderia Torino, sponsoring others to race. By the end of the 1930s he was a wealthy industrialist whose interests included manufacturing sporting goods. His organization was called Consorzio Industriale Sportivo Italia, from which the name Cisitalia is derived.

After World War II Dusio realized his idea of building competition cars, utilizing the considerable talents of ex-Fiat engineer Dante Giacosa to design the new car. This was to be a spartan racer easy to mass-produce and based, with that company's consent, on Fiat components.

Giacosa designed his own chassis for a Fiat engine and in mid-1945 Dusio took on Dr. Giovanni Savonuzzi, also previously with Fiat, to organize production. This car, the D46, had immediate racing success, considerably boosting Cisitalia's sporting reputation.

Various other prototype bodies were produced around this time, by Farina, Vignale and Pininfarina. High placings in the 1947 Mille Miglia brought increased orders that Cisitalia had trouble meeting, but Dusio had dreams of entering the Grand Prix arena. Through Carlo Abarth in Turin, Dusio contacted Dr. Ferdinand Porsche who designed a suitable supercharged car for him. Working alongside Porsche were competition engineers Dr. Eberan von Eberhorst and Ing. Karl Rabe.

Unfortunately, the project soon exceeded its budget, and when Savonuzzi's fears that the final costs would be five times the initial estimate were ignored, he resigned. Dusio replaced him with Rudolf Hrushka and continued at the expense of all else. By 1949 he was bankrupt.

Dusio then sold the remains of his company to Automotores Argentinos – Autoar – in the hope of reviving the marque with government backing, but only Cisitalia-badged Willys-type vehicles were built. In 1952 Dusio tried again in Italy, with his son Carlo, producing an unsuccessful series of rebodied Fiats. The last Cisitalias, built between 1961 and 1965, were the generally unremarkable small-engined Coupé Tourism Specials.

Below: The bodywork on this 1947 Cisitalia 202 coupé was by Pininfarina. The engine was a 1090cc Fiat four-cylinder, tuned to produce 60bhp. Few were made before financial troubles overtook the company.

Citroën

France
1919 to date

André Citroën was a graduate of the élite *Ecole Polytechnique* in Paris who was taken on as Chief Engineer by the Mors concern in 1908 after spending time in the French Army as an engineering officer. His genius lay in production methods, and he demonstrated this by streamlining the Mors assembly lines.

Above: 1922 Type A 5CV two-seater

Above: 1922 Type B2 'Caddy' roadster

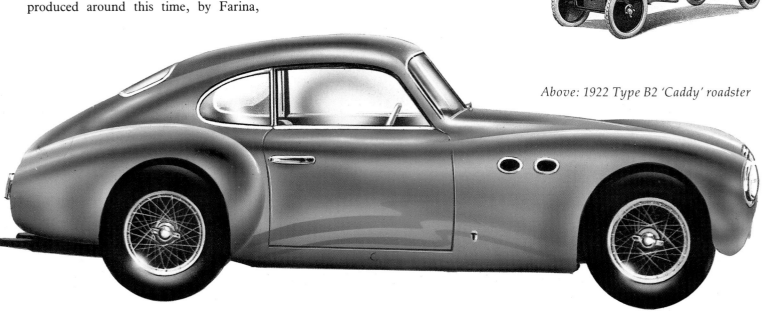

But Citroën was anxious to set up on his own and, in 1913, he started his own company to manufacture gearwheels, in particular of the double-helical design which would later be reflected in the chevrons adopted as the Citroën car company's emblem. During World War I, the French Government helped him to buy a large factory in Paris where he applied his manufacturing flair to the mass-production of shells for the French Army.

After the war, Citroën devoted this factory and its modern American machine-tools to car production. He started in 1919 with the type A, designed in association with Jules Salomon (who had already worked for Le Zebre and

Above: Citroën London taxi, mid-1920s

Above right: 1925 B12 all-steel Torpedo
Right: 1926 B14 Coupé de Ville taxi

would later move on to Rosengart). The type A was intended to be a car for Everyman, and Citroën mass-produced it in far larger numbers than his rivals could achieve. This lasted until 1921, when it was replaced with the type B2, an improved version with a larger engine.

As before, a variety of bodies could be had, running costs were cheap and the volume-production enabled Citroën to keep the purchase price low. In 1921 Citroën also launched the small type C, broadly similar to the B2 in design and intended to appeal to women drivers. This was another huge success, but was withdrawn in 1926 when Citroën recognized that there was more profit to be made from his larger cars.

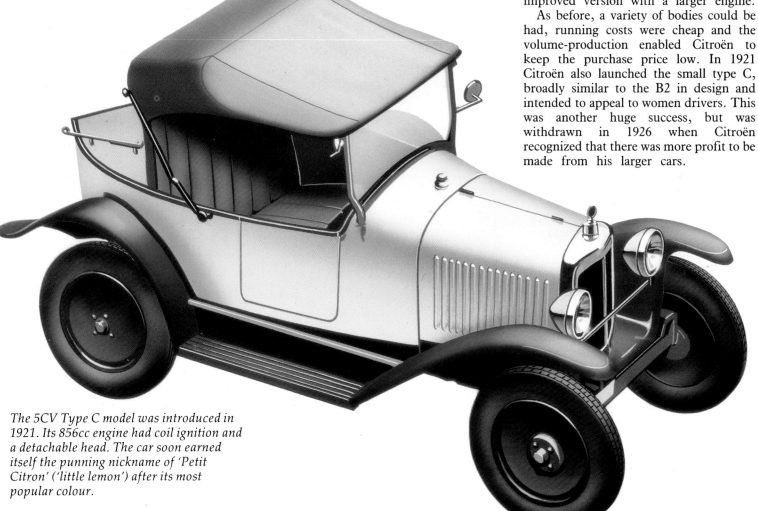

The 5CV Type C model was introduced in 1921. Its 856cc engine had coil ignition and a detachable head. The car soon earned itself the punning nickname of 'Petit Citron' ('little lemon') after its most popular colour.

By this stage, Citroën had already branched out far beyond car manufacture. In 1923, he had set up his own taxi company, using exclusively his own B2 taxis. A thriving commercial-vehicle range was also in production, having grown gradually out of the B2 cars, and from 1932 the *Société des Transports André Citroën* ran a vast network of bus and coach services all over France – using, of course, single-deck buses built by Citroën.

Such services, besides bringing additional revenue to the Citroën empire, also functioned as a form of advertising, which was a sphere in which André Citroën excelled. Going far further than his contemporaries, he advertised his products not only in the usual specialist publications but also in the national press; he arranged for the company name to be written in the sky over Paris by an aeroplane in 1922; and he displayed it in lights on all four sides of the Eiffel Tower at night. Throughout the 1920s and early 1930s, he even sent convoys of Citroën vehicles – mostly the half-track *Kégresse* models – across the most impenetrable deserts in order to demonstrate their ruggedness and durability.

Seeking still-more efficient production methods, Citroën signed an agreement with the American Budd Company to produce all-steel bodies under licence. The first such bodies appeared on B10 models in 1924, and the B range was progressively improved until its demise in 1928. The inherent design flexibility of the later models allowed Citroën to produce a large number of variants of the same basic model relatively cheaply.

The B range was replaced by the C4 (four-cylinder) and C6 (six-cylinder) models, which showed strong American design influence. These lasted until 1932 when a new 'Rosalie' range arrived, with simpler and stronger bodies based on a common new design. Citroën was able to juggle trim and specification levels and, approving the offerings of outside coachbuilders, catalogued no fewer than 83 different models.

Up to this point, Citroën models had been largely conventional in their design, but an individualistic streak came to the fore in 1934, when the Rosalies were replaced by the revolutionary *Traction Avant* (literally, 'front-wheel-drive').

Above: 1925 Type C
Left: 1932 C6 coach

Left: 1928 C4 four-door saloon
Above: 1928 Rosalie 15CV saloon

The 1934 Traction Avant featured an all-steel monocoque with the engine and transmission mounted on a detachable subframe, front-wheel-drive, and all-independent suspension by torsion bars.

Again offering a wide range of variants based on a common design, this was the first mass-produced car in Europe to feature chassisless monocoque construction, independent suspension on all four wheels, and front-wheel-drive. Its overhead-valve wet-liner engine was also new. This outstandingly successful vehicle remained available until 1957, but the cost of getting it into production drove Citroën to bankruptcy and the company was bought at the end of 1934 by its principal creditors, the Michelin tyre firm. André Citroën himself died a year later.

A new small Citroën was introduced in 1948. This was the 2CV, with an air-cooled flat-twin engine driving the front wheels and an interconnected suspension system. It offered ingenious solutions to the problems of cheap motoring, and soon became a cult car, continuing in production for the next four decades. Even after French production ceased in 1988, 2CV manufacture continued in some of Citroën's overseas plants. It had been joined in 1961 by the larger Ami and in 1967 by the more sophisticated Dyane, both of which were based on the same design. Both, however, ceased production in the 1970s.

Meanwhile, the introduction in 1955 of the new large Citroën had again demonstrated the company's commitment to advanced technology. The futuristically styled S saloon had high pressure hydraulic circuits for its self-levelling suspension, brakes, steering and gear-change, and broke new ground with its revolutionary 'base-unit' construction, consisting of a steel inner skeleton to which unstressed outer panels were bolted. The D was also the first production car in the world to have front-wheel disc brakes as standard; in 1967 it pioneered auxiliary headlights which turned with the steering to light the road on bends; and, in 1969, the DS21 version became the first French production car to have electronic fuel-injection.

Citroën experimented with rotary engines in the late 1960s and early 1970s, sharing development with the German NSU company, but the production cars of the 1970s retained their conventional piston engines. The GS of 1971 fitted between the D range and the small 2CV/Ami/Dyane models, offering a

Above: 1933 Rosalie 8CV Faux-Cabriolet

Above right: 1934 Traction Avant 11CV saloon

Reproduced with permission
© Haynes Publishing Group, 1981

Above: 1955 DS19 saloon
Below: 1948 375cc 2CV
Bottom: 1959 DS Safari estate

Above: 1961 British-built Bijou
Below: 1961 Ami-6 saloon

Left: The 2CV was designed as a car for French rural communities and put ease of maintenance, practicality and frugality above all other qualities. The 1948 original was still readily recognizable in this 1970s 602cc version.

light-alloy, air-cooled, overhead-valve flat-four engine, disc brakes and the hydropneumatic suspension among its many refinements, while the low-volume SM grand tourer of 1970 added a high-performance Maserati engine gained through a short-lived link with the Italian manufacturer to the characteristic Citroën technology.

The SM previewed some of the features which would be seen in the CX saloons, introduced in 1974 to replace the D models. This included a controversial steering system with power-assisted self-centring. In appearance, the CX was less idiosyncratic than recent Citroëns had been, although this was perhaps more a result of other manufacturers catching up than of Citroën regressing. On its introduction, the CX won Europe's Car of the Year award, plus a safety award and a further award for body design, thus becoming the first car ever to claim all three awards at once. A wide range of variants followed, including the first diesel-powered Citroën in 1975; and the range remained in production until 1989, when it was replaced by the distinctive, Bertone-styled XM. Notable for its

The 1955 D-series again brought advanced technology to a mass-produced saloon car. High-pressure hydraulics powered brakes, steering, gearchange and self-levelling suspension. The styling was futuristic and remained unique.

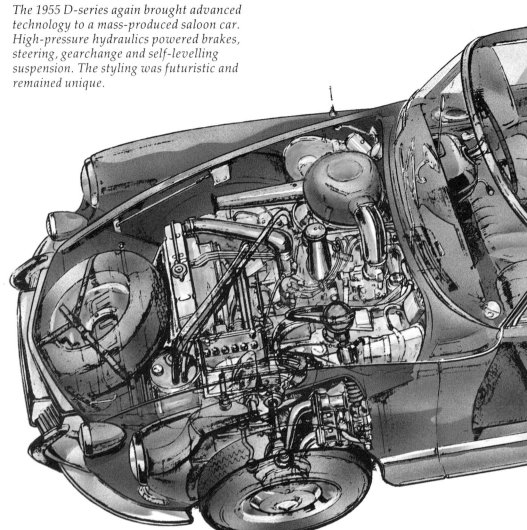

Above: 1971 GS saloon

Above: 1972 Dyane 6

Below: 1974 SM coupé

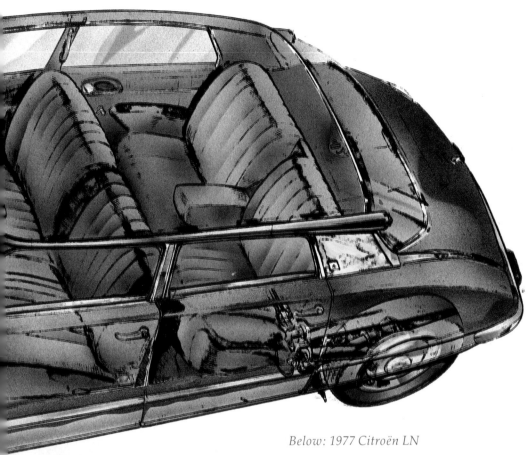

'hydractive' suspension system – which automatically adjusts spring and damper settings to allow an absorbent ride over poor surfaces but sharply composed handling through corners – this was also acclaimed Car of the Year, in 1990.

Citroën was bought by former rival Peugeot in 1975, and the marque began to lose some of its individuality. The small LN and later LNA models simply fitted Citroën's air-cooled twin-cylinder engine into a Peugeot body shell; and the Visa initially added the air-cooled flat-twin and a new body to a Peugeot floorpan, later taking on a four-cylinder Peugeot engine option as well.

In the 1980s, however, this cross-fertilization between the two companies was no longer so apparent. The first new model was the BX of 1983, which replaced the GS range. Although the engines were conventional designs from the Peugeot stable, the BX had Citroën's characteristic self-levelling hydropneumatic suspension and disc brakes all round. Styling – by Lamborghini, Miura and Countach designer Marcello Cardini while he was at Bertone – was distinctive if somewhat less outrageous than Citroën designs of recent years had tended to be. And, most importantly, the BX sold extremely well.

Below: 1977 Citroën LN

Production of the 2CV for Citroën's main markets finally ceased in 1988, but the model which was to replace it had arrived the previous year. Once again, Peugeot engines were used, and the car fitted into the existing 'supermini' bracket rather than creating its own market niche as the 2CV had done 40 years earlier. Nevertheless, the AX offered an attractive combination of style, practicality and cheap running costs. Light commercials based on the Visa car range were also available into the late 1980s, and Citroën continued to manufacture or assemble cars in several foreign countries, while some Citroën-based designs were being built under licence in eastern European countries.

Above: 1979 Visa Super

Above: 1979 CX2400 Pallas

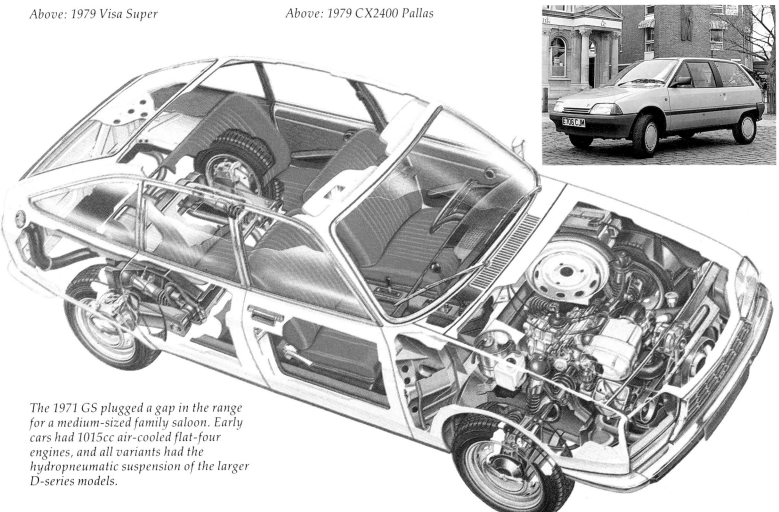

The 1971 GS plugged a gap in the range for a medium-sized family saloon. Early cars had 1015cc air-cooled flat-four engines, and all variants had the hydropneumatic suspension of the larger D-series models.

Left: 1987 AX 11TRE hatchback   *Above: 1979 GS Club Break (estate car)*   *Below: 1989 XM saloon*

As well as producing more conventional models, Citroën also persisted with developing hydropneumatic suspension. In the Xantia (the BX replacement, launched in 1992), Citroën engineers fitted an active suspension that cancelled out body roll completely. This system, known as Activa by Citroën, was usually fitted to the larger 2.0- or 3.0-litre engine models.

For those who were frightened by all the traditional Citroën plumbing, there were more conventional models, such as the ZX, also launched in 1992 with normal, coil-sprung suspension. A sales success, the ZX was also available as an estate.

The little AX continued well into the 1990s and was still sold following the launch of its replacement, the Saxo, in 1995. The Saxo was little more than a Peugeot 106 with a new nose and tail. The engine range was the same as the Peugeot's and included a hot 118bhp 1.6-litre unit for the very sporting Saxo VTS.

The quirky XM remained relatively unchanged as Citroën's slow-selling, top-of-the range model.

A new departure for the company was the launch of the Synergie, or Evasion, as it was known on some markets. This people carrier, Citroën's first, was the result of a collaboration between Peugeot/Citroën and Fiat/Lancia, who all had their own versions of the same car.

Right: By Citroën standards, the ZX was a very conventional car. It was also the company's best-selling car. In 1991, the Rally Raid version won the Paris-Dakar Rally with a comfortable lead

Above: The XM was a traditonal Citroën with strange looks and even stranger mechanics. Unfortunately, it wasn't a big seller

Left: The Berlingo was Citroën's answer to Renault's successful Mégane Scenic in the new mini MPV class

*Above: The Citroën Xantia was the first
production car to have active suspension*

*Above: The Saxo replaced the AX in 1996. This
is the top-of-the-range model, the VTS*

*Above: The Synergie, or Evasion, was built in
conjunction with Peugeot, Fiat and Lancia*

Clyno

Great Britain
1922–1929

The Wolverhampton firm of Clyno – originally motorcycle manufacturers – began assembling cars in 1922. The 10.8hp Clyno used the dependable 1.4-litre Coventry-Climax engine. This drove the rear wheels via a torque tube, a cone-type clutch and the company's own three-speed gearbox.

Clyno earned a justifiable reputation for reliability, and by 1926 up to 350 10.8s were being produced each week. By this time, the car had gained a differential, plain (instead of roller-type) engine bearings, four-wheel braking, and semi-elliptic leaf-spring suspension. The 10.8 ('Eleven') was built in several versions, including a high-specification Royal model.

Clyno's Frank Smith aimed his company's vehicles at the market dominated by the huge rival firm of Morris and, indeed, the 10.8hp Clyno challenged the Cowley of the same era for sales, with virtually identical pricing and improved equipment. The saloon version of the Clyno had four doors and four-wheel brakes, for example, compared with two of each on the equivalent Morris Cowley.

In an attempt to repeat this success against the larger Morris Oxford, a Clyno 12/28 model was introduced, based on the short-lived 1924 11.9hp, and the company's premises were expanded.

Unfortunately, by the late 1920s Clynos were beginning to look a little dated, and sales started to decline.

Problems multiplied because Frank Smith tried to build cars down to a price – specifically as close as possible to the magical £100 figure. In Clyno's attempt to achieve this, the fabric-bodied Nine, introduced in 1928, was made available in a very basic form as the Century but it was not a success. This did not help an already under-capitalized firm, nor did the withdrawal by the distributors, Rootes.

Although Clyno built larger models, notably the 12/35, and had even

Above: The popular Clyno 10.8hp (1926)   *Below: 1926 Clyno Royale*

experimented with a 22hp, straight-eight-cylinder prototype, the writing was on the wall. The company did not survive beyond 1929, having by this time built some 36,000 cars.

Above: One of the larger Clynos, the 12/35hp, like this 1927 example, performed well but did not sell in large numbers
Below: 1927 Clyno 10.8hp

Continental

U.S.A.
1955–1960

The Continental marque was produced by a separate division of the Ford Motor Co., which was created in 1955 with the aim of producing luxury, up-market cars to compete with Cadillac.

Since production of the original Lincoln Continental ceased in 1948, Ford had been under pressure to produce a successor and, in 1956, the Continental Mark II was introduced.

The Special Products Division, as it was known, was headed by William Clay Ford, younger brother of Henry Ford II who commissioned several outside consultants to produce design proposals for the new car. The management committee finally selected the design from the Special Products Division, and Harley F. Copp, chief engineer, designed a unique chassis for the new model that was low enough between the axles to give a high seating position but without a high roof line.

Designed primarily as an 'image' car rather than a profit maker, the Mark II was flawlessly hand-built, had graceful lines and was priced at U.S. $10,000. The car was powered by a specially assembled Lincoln V8 engine and three-speed automatic transmission.

Although there was initial enthusiasm for the Mark II, it did not sell very well, and G.M. was still the leader in the luxury-car market. A lower-priced 'new' Continental model, dubbed the Mark III, was available from 1959 to 1960, based on the standard Lincoln model, but even at U.S. $6,000 this did not sell very well either. In view of the disappointing sales, the four-door Berline and convertible models were never produced.

In 1959, in line with an upper management decision, the 'Continental' marque was dropped and the car became a Lincoln as it had been before, and Continental as a separate division was gone by late 1960, merged with Lincoln and Mercury.

Cord

U.S.A.
1929–1937

Cord entered the car scene at the end of the 1920s. This rakish American marque was launched in 1929 by Erret Lobban Cord, who gave the U.S.A. its first front-wheel-drive car in reasonable numbers.

As a teenager Cord had made and lost considerable sums of money buying and selling used Model T Fords in and around Los Angeles, California. Legend has it that he was down on his luck with only 20 dollars in his pocket and he decided to try for better fortune in Chicago. There he got himself a job as a salesman for a Moon dealership, selling the Victory model which became extremely popular.

His talents as a salesman in his early twenties saw him earn terrific commission, and his wages were reported to be 15 times those of a skilled worker.

When sales of the Victory model began to decline Cord showed an interest in the Auburn Automobile Company which, in 1924, was in the hands of a receiver.

He was given the chance to reorganize the company and within a year he had restored its fortunes and expanded the manufacturing plant at Auburn, Indiana.

Cord then decided he wanted to build a car bearing his name, and the Cord L-29 was introduced into Auburn showrooms in October 1929. This front-wheel-drive car, with a straight-eight-cylinder 125bhp Lycoming FDA engine of 4.9 litres, created tremendous interest. Resembling the J-series Duesenberg, the exclusive Cord was long and sleek. It was available in four styles – Brougham, Sedan, Convertible Cabriolet and Convertible Phaeton.

The car remained in production until 1932 (the worst sales year in the U.S.A. since the end of World War I), some 4,429 having been built during that time. Magnificent though it was, however, it had an Achilles' heel of universal-joint failure because of the front-wheel-drive.

The Depression of the early 1930s did not help matters and production of Cord

Above: 1929 Cord L29

cars was not taken up again until 1936 when Cord brought out an all-new 810 model designed by Gordon Buehrig.

Originally conceived as a 'small' Duesenberg, the new machine continued the front-wheel-drive crusade and was powered by a 4.7-litre Lycoming V8 engine giving 125bhp at 3,500rpm.

A supercharged version, the 812 giving 195bhp, was introduced in 1937, but these stunning but expensive new models were not sales successes. Perhaps one of the reasons was that they were too modern for their day, for in later years they gained great appreciation and esteem, the design

being cited for its beauty by the Museum of Modern Art in New York.

Also some small companies made replicas starting with Glenn Pray of Oklahoma who used a flat-six Chevrolet Corvair engine to power his glassfibre homage to the 810/812 series which came to a halt in 1937 after only 2,320 had been built. Pray's replica, made from 1964–72, stayed faithful to the front-wheel-drive concept.

The passing of the Cord signified the passing of a flamboyant time in American

The Cord L-29 was introduced in 1929. The front-wheel-drive system came from engineering genius Harry Miller who had designed a fwd racing car in 1925. The engine was a 4894cc Lycoming straight eight.

automotive history. The victim of high prices and a lengthy depression, the Cord was part of an Auburn-Cord-Duesenberg triumvirate which produced some of the most magnificent machines in the history of motoring.

Former racing driver Cord, who earned a reputation for buying companies 'on the cheap', had acquired Duesenberg in 1928 plus the Lycoming engine factory. Auburn production ceased in 1936, and Duesenberg joined the Cord marque when it disappeared in 1937.

In that year Cord himself is reported to have gone bankrupt, but the dynamic entrepreneur held on to his Lycoming engine factory and supplied aero-engines during World War II. The man who made and lost fortunes and shaped some of the world's most stylish cars died in 1974.

Top: 1936 Cord 810 Sportsman   *Above: 1937 Cord 812 Phaeton*   *Below: 1937 Cord 812 Sedan*

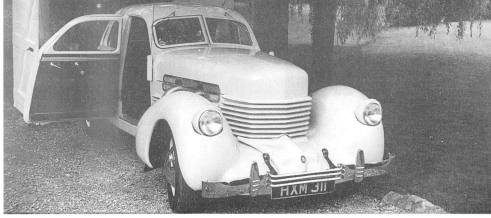

Crossley

Great Britain
1904–1937

Crossley made stationary engines before building vehicles, but the first Crossley car – a 22hp four-cylinder machine with Mercedes-like design and chain-drive – appeared in 1904. This car and its successors, the 20/28 and 40hp models, were designed by J. S. Critchley (from Daimler) and W. M. MacFarland.

The Manchester-based company turned from chain- to shaft-drive in 1906, and had used four-wheel brakes by 1910. For this year two new models were introduced – the 12/14 and the four-litre 20hp, both designed by G. Hubert Woods and A. W. Reeves. These cars developed into 15hp and 20/25hp models, which were produced by a new subsidiary company – Crossley Motors Ltd. – set up for manufacturing vehicles.

In 1913 a 15hp 'Shelsley' model was introduced, with a monobloc L-head engine.

Many Crossley 20/25s were used by the War Department during World War I. After the war, the 20/25 was developed

Top: Ex. World War I 4½-litre Crossley 25/30
Left: The reliable Crossley 20/25

Below: 1925/6 Crossley 12/14

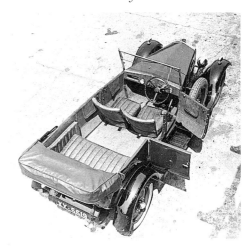

into the larger, 4½-litre 25/30.

A new Crossley for 1921 was the 19.6hp model. Designed by T. D. Wishart, the car featured a detachable cylinder head, as did the sports version, the 20/70hp, a heavy car, but guaranteed by the manufacturers to achieve 75mph (120 km/h).

In 1923, Crossley offered a 12/14hp model, but by 1926 the company had turned from sidevalve fours to overhead-valve sixes, and the 2.6-litre 18/50 emerged. Two years later the engine was enlarged to 3.2 litres (now rated at 20.9hp), this version being made for some nine years.

In 1928, Crossley introduced a two-litre 15.7hp saloon, with a sports ('Shelsley') version available from1929. The 15.7 was built into the 1930s, the engine also being used by Lagonda for its 16/80.

In 1932 the Crossley Ten was announced. It had an 1100cc Coventry-Climax engine and a preselector gearbox. Another fascinating car was the independently sprung, rear-engined Crossley-Burney of 1934, powered by the six-cylinder, two-litre 15.7hp engine. Sadly, only two dozen were built.

In 1935 the attractive Regis – in four-cylinder, 1100cc 'Ten', or six-cylinder, 1500cc form – was introduced. However, even these were discontinued after 1937.

Above: The Crossley 19.6hp, 1921 on
Left: An early Crossley 22hp

Left: 1907 Crossley 30/40hp
Below: 1933 Crossley Torquay Ten

Cunningham

U.S.A. 1907–1937; 1951– 1955

There were two quite unrelated Cunningham marques. One specialized in building high-class carriages and cars while the other built competition sports cars. James Cunningham, Son and Co. of Rochester, New York, had been carriage builders since 1842, but it was not until 1907 that their first car, electrically powered, was unveiled. This was quickly succeeded by petrol-driven cars using Continental as well as their own four-cylinder engines, and by 1915 the Cunningham cars had become larger, more powerful (thanks to their new V8 engine) and much more expensive.

The cars were highly rated and well able to compete with the prestigious American Rolls-Royce and the best of the Packards and McFarlans, and over the next decade the luxurious Cunninghams occupied a small but profitable niche in the American market. The company also manufactured high-quality funeral vehicles and ambulances. However, during the Depression sales began to decline with the last cars being built in 1931, although the company continued to make special bodies for other peoples' chassis until 1937 when the company finally closed down.

Briggs Swift Cunningham, born in 1907, was a wealthy sportsman with interests in ocean sailing and motor racing and most of his sports cars were built with competition in mind, particularly the Le Mans 24-Hour race.

The 1951 prototype C-1 sports car, with its V8 Cadillac engine, was quickly followed by open- and closed-body C-2Rs powered by 300bhp Chrysler engines. Although three of these cars failed to finish in the 1951 Le Mans, the following year saw a C-4R driven by Cunningham himself take fourth place, while in 1953 Cunninghams came third, seventh and tenth. These competition cars had stubby, purposeful bodies designed by Robert Blake (later of Jaguar) and were strong and powerful, as were the production cars, such as the fine-looking 1952 GT with its 200bhp Chrysler engine.

One of Cunningham's greatest achievements was an outright win in the 1953 Sebring 12-hour race in Florida, but this was not to be repeated at Le Mans and in 1955 Cunningham decided to call it a day and the manufacture of his cars ceased. However, Briggs Cunningham did continue racing other marques including Lister, Jaguar, Maserati and Chevrolet, with a GT category win in a Corvette in the 1960 Le Mans. In later years he was famous for his extensive collection of cars.

Above: 1912 Model 'J' Cunningham Limousine

Below: For the 1952 Le Mans 24-Hour race, Cunningham entered three new vehicles: two C4R open cars and a special C4RK coupé. The cars were big and strong, with 325bhp available from the Chrysler V8 engine.

Daewoo

South Korea
1980 to date

A new entrant to the world car market during the 1990s was Daewoo. The Korean company, which began in textiles, had been building cars for the home market since 1980 but only started selling cars elsewhere in the mid-1990s. By the time the cars came to Europe, Daewoo was already building more vehicles per year than the largest British manufacturer. It was the 33rd biggest company in the world (bigger than Coca-Cola), building everything from oil tankers to aircraft and diggers.

At first, Daewoo set its sights on Europe, hoping to establish itself there. The cars were nothing special, simply repackaged Vauxhalls and Opels, but the way in which the cars were sold was completely new. Rather than building up a dealer network where Daewoo

Above: Daewoo Nexia three-door hatchback

Below: The Nexia four-door saloon

would have limited control over customer care and sales, the company sold cars direct at a fixed, no haggling, price which included all servicing and consumable service parts for three years. Using such techniques, Daewoo expected to be selling 200,000 cars a year across Europe.

This method of marketing cars was thought to be so effective that rival dealers started a boycott, refusing to take Daewoos in part exchange. No other manufacturer could compete without incurring losses.

The cars proved to be reliable but could never be described as exciting. The Nexia, based on the Opel Kadett/Vauxhall Astra, received a decent face-lift so that it at least looked passably modern, as did the Vauxhall Cavalier-based Espero.

Finally, having proved to itself that cars were worthwhile business, Daewoo launched new models, designed completely in-house, in 1997, and looked to be on target for an even brighter future.

Above: Daewoo Lanos, Nubira and Leganza   *Below: the Vauxhall Cavalier-based Espero*

DAF

Holland
1958–1975

DAF of Eindhoven, Holland, began building cars in 1958, following many years of manufacturing commercial and military vehicles. The company's first small saloon car was powered by an air-cooled, flat-twin engine of 590cc, developing 22bhp and driving the rear wheels through belt-operated 'Variomatic' transmission, which employed a centrifugal clutch and twin vee-belts. This gave constantly varying drive ratios to suit the prevailing road conditions. The DAF was first exported to the U.K. in 1961.

Further models were announced in 1962 – the 750 and the Daffodil, with 30bhp engines which allowed a top speed of around 65mph (104km/h).

In late 1966 the larger, Michelotti-styled DAF 44 was introduced, with a longer-stroke version of the flat-twin engine, now of 844cc and producing 40bhp. This gave a top speed approaching

Below: 1965 Variomatic racing car
Bottom: 1959 33, with air-cooled engine

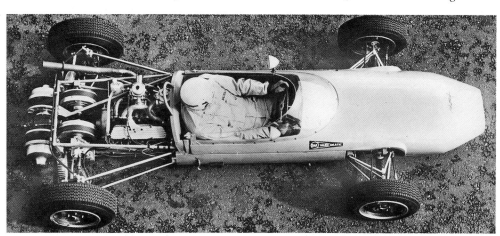

80mph (128km/h). Stability was improved by widening the track and lengthening the wheel-base.

In early 1968, the DAF 55 was announced. This retained the belt-drive transmission, but was powered by a modified four-cylinder Renault engine of 1108cc, giving 50bhp and 140km/h (87mph). This model also featured 12-volt electrics, earlier cars having six-volt systems. By 1969, estate-car variants of the 44 and 55 were available as well as a 55 Coupé.

A Marathon version of the 55 was announced during 1971, the model celebrating the success of DAFs entered in the 1968 London-to-Sydney Marathon. The production cars were uprated to give some 13bhp more than the standard 55 models, and cruised comfortably at speeds above 128km/h (80mph).

In 1972 the DAF 66 Series was introduced to replace the 55 models. The new cars had revised styling and a new, plate-type automatic clutch, while revisions were made to the 1108cc engine to give quieter operation and a little more power. A Marathon version of the 66 was produced, with improvements similar to those made on the Marathon 55. A 1300cc

Left: 1967 DAF 44 estate car
Above: 1974 55 Coupé Marathon

Above right: DAF 66 Coupé Marathon

Below: The 750cc Daffodil was introduced in 1962, and like the earlier 600cc-engined car featured DAF's 'Variomatic' transmission.

66 was introduced in 1973, although the 1100 model was still available.

In 1975 DAF ceased production, but

Volvo took over and built its own, restyled version of the DAF 66, with the 1300cc engine and servo-operated clutch.

Daimler

Great Britain
1896 to date

The Daimler Motor Syndicate was formed in 1893 to build the German car of the same name under licence, but the British and German concerns went their separate ways after 1898. The first Daimlers were imported, but the Coventry factory soon began to turn out twin-cylinder models and eventually a whole range of types.

From 1904, the company began to concentrate on large and powerful four-cylinder cars with chain drive to the wheels. Before long, it was making some of the biggest and best British cars, with its prestige well established thanks to the purchase of a Daimler in 1900 by the then

Left: 1898 model, probably imported
Above: 1904 28hp Landaulette

Below: 1923 30hp Landaulette

Above: 1909 four-cylinder tourer

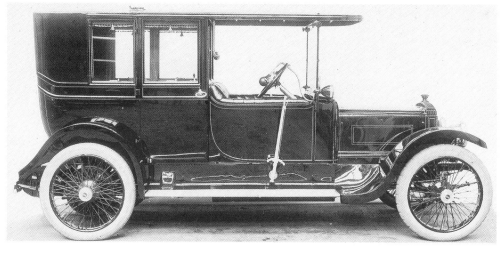

Prince of Wales, later King Edward VII.
Royal patronage would stay with the
marque until the 1950s.

Major changes took place in 1909 and
1910. In the former, Daimler changed over
completely from poppet-valve engines to
Knight sleeve-valve designs; in the latter,
the company was bought out by the BSA
Group. Thus began a period in which the
Daimler name signified large, smooth and
silent cars, which were dignified rather
than sporting. There were no more
four-cylinder cars after World War I
(except for the short-lived '20' of 1922),
and in 1927 the company announced the
fabulous Double-Six, with a V12 engine of
7.1 litres. This was the first of many V12s,

Below: 1911 20hp Doctor's coupé

Top: 20hp Landaulette, built around 1912
Above: 1914 45hp 'special' for India
Below: 1921 Light Thirty

which ranged in size down to 1.9 litres and
would remain in production until 1938.

The Daimler car range alone was
enormous; but, in addition, there had been
well-respected buses since 1908, and the
company marketed small cars under the
BSA name. A range of medium-sized cars

was added under the Lanchester name after that company was bought out in 1931. This diversification gave the company a sound commercial footing, but by the end of the 1930s it had abandoned the very top of the market to Rolls-Royce.

The Daimlers of the 1930s were characterized by Wilson-type preselector gearboxes which drove through a fluid flywheel, and this transmission was standard on all models until the 1950s. Independent front suspension appeared in 1938, but the stately Double-Six had ceased production a year earlier, its engine already reduced to 6½-litres. For 1939, the largest Daimler was the 4½-litre straight-eight first seen in 1936.

Above: 1930 Double-Six
Below: 1931 Light straight eight

Below: 1932 Fifteen Sports Coupé

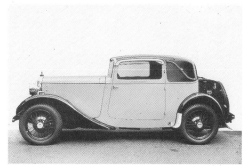

Above: 1938 Light Twenty saloon
Below: 1939 DB18 saloon

Above: 1949 DE39 5.5-litre

Above: 1957 Conquest drophead coupé

After World War II, the pre-war 15 was revived with some modifications, and there were two new limousine models, one with the six-cylinder engine originally designed for an armoured car and the other with a straight-eight of 5½-litres. Lanchester production was also resumed, along with a successful range of bus and coach chassis.

The Daimlers of the 1950s were conservatively styled, although the company remained in the public eye through a series of flamboyant Show cars commissioned by its Chairman, Sir Bernard Docker. The Conquest, Majestic, and 'One-O-Four' models were well-equipped owner-driver saloons, and there was also a sports two/three-seater. After

Above: 1955 Regency Mk. II

Below: The 1959 SP250 sports car had a glassfibre body and a 140bhp overhead-valve V8 engine of 2547cc. Top speed was 197km/h (123mph). It was a departure for Daimler, and one which the firm never followed up.

1956, automatic transmission became an alternative to the fluid flywheel, and 1958's 3.8-litre Majestic Major had automatic transmission as standard. A year later, the new SP250 sports car came with either a synchromesh gearbox or a conventional automatic only.

The SP250 had a 2½-litre V8 engine, designed by Edward Turner along with a 4½-litre V8 for use in the limousine models. But, in 1960, the company was bought out by Jaguar, and that company's influence gradually came to dominate. In 1962 the 2½-litre V8 was fitted to a Mark II Jaguar body shell, and the last Majestic Major was built in 1967. After 1969, all Daimler saloons were Jaguars with trim and equipment variations. The name still survives, but the only really distinctive model is a limousine with a special body on a Jaguar floorpan and running gear.

Jaguar itself was purchased by Ford Motor Company in 1989.

Left: 1962 SP250 sports
Below left: 1968 DS420 limousine
Below centre: 1969 Sovereign
Below right: 1974 DS420 Landaulette

Above: 1977 Vanden Plas 4.2-litre
Left: 1973 Double-Six coupé

Darracq

France
1896–1920

Alexandre Darracq had a great passion for mechanical objects and over a 20-year period he designed and built a wide range of bicycles, tricycles and cars; and yet, incredibly, he did not like driving and hated being driven.

Darracq was born in 1855 in Bordeaux, south-western France, of Basque parents and he first came to prominence around 1891 when, with his partner Jean Aucoc, he formed the Gladiator cycle company, quickly cashing in on the current bicycle boom. However, some five years later his company was bought out by Adolphe Clément, and Darracq turned his hand to designing electric cabs which proved to be a complete failure.

He had more luck with his tricycles inspired by Léon Bollée and on the strength of their success he paid £10,000 for the manufacturing rights of Bollée's latest four-wheeler. This belt-driven machine was an unmitigated failure, however, with recurrent ignition problems and badly designed steering.

The year 1900 saw a change in Darracq's fortunes with the introduction of a more conventional and very handsome 6.5hp voiturette. The car had a 785cc single-cylinder engine, a propeller shaft driving a bevel-gear rear axle and a three-speed steering-column gear-change. By 1903 twin- and four-cylinder models had been added to the range, while the following year the multi-cylinder cars sported a pressed-steel platform chassis.

During this period the marque performed quite well on the racing scene, with the company's V8-engined sprint car being capable of reaching nearly 190km/h (118mph), making it one of the fastest cars of its day. Racing success continued with the works team taking second, third and seventh places in the 1908 Isle of Man Tourist Trophy race, but by this time Darracq had found a new interest in the developing sport of flying, and within two years his Suresnes factory was building light aero-engines.

The following years were marred by a series of disasters beginning with the production of steam buses which failed to sell, followed by the demise of the Milan operation with which the company had hoped to take a share of the developing

Above: 1903 20hp racer

Below: Darracqs performed well in long-distance races with their V8 engines, and were capable of reaching 193km/h (120mph), making them among the fastest cars of their day. This is a 1904 racing model.

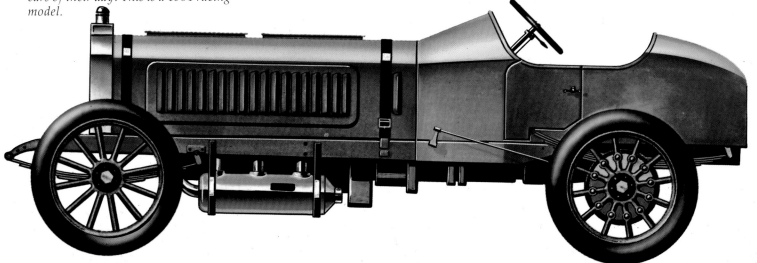

Italian market. The downward trend continued, and despite the injection of some British capital the new range of models introduced in 1912, many of which were fitted with the Henroid rotary-valve engine, did nothing to stem the company's sinking fortunes. That same year Alexandre Darracq resigned and in 1931, at the age of 76, he died.

The company was taken over by Yorkshireman Owen Clegg who introduced a new range of cars, the Clegg-Darracqs based on his own successful Rover Twelve design. They were a great success and by the autumn of 1914 the Suresnes factory was turning out 70 cars a week, with many of the big

Top: 1903 40hp racer

Above left: 1904 8hp single-cylinder
Above right: 1904 100hp Darracq
Above: 1914 Clegg-Darracq four-cylinder

Left: 1907 16/18 tourer

four-litre models going to the French Army.

A new 4.6-litre V8 model was announced in 1919, yet despite its advanced specification – a four-speed gearbox and four-wheel braking – it did not sell well and in 1920 the ailing company was taken over by Sunbeam-Talbot. During the next two decades the cars were sold as Talbots in France and Darracqs or Talbot-Darracqs in Britain and the Empire.

Left: 1906 10/12hp
Below: 1914 16hp

Above right: 1919 4-litre tourer
Right: 1954 Lago Talbot coupé

Top: 1922 16hp
Above: 1926 12/32

Below: In 1920, the ailing Darracq company was taken over by Sunbeam Talbot, and the cars were subsequently badged as Talbot-Darracqs. This 1920 six-cylinder 25hp A-type was a Darracq design, however.

Datsun

Japan
1912-1983

Many people regard Datsun as a company of the 1970s and 1980s but, in fact, its origins date back to as long ago as 1912.

American-trained engineer Masujiro Hashimoto founded the Kwaishinsha Motor Works in Tokyo and built a prototype small car. Little is known about it. However, another small car followed two years later.

Hashimoto's financiers were called K. Den, R. Aoyama and A. Takeuchi and the car was called the DAT, using the initials of their surnames. The name was particularly appropriate because 'dat' is the Japanese word for hare.

The DAT 31 came in 1915, featuring a two-litre, four-cylinder engine. The next year's model was the DAT 41 which had a 2.3-litre power unit.

Production of everything except wheels, tyres and magnetos was carried out in Japan. After a modest production run, the company turned to trucks in 1926.

A year earlier, Kwaishinsha had changed its name to DAT Motor Co., later moving to Osaka to merge with the Jitsuyo Jidosha Seizo Co.

That company continued to make the Lila light car for a short period after the

Above: 1951 Thrift four-door saloon
Below: 1951 De Luxe four-door saloon

merger. It was popular with taxi drivers in Japan because of its exceptionally narrow track, and followed an earlier three-wheeler designed by William Gorham, an American engineer who was living in Japan.

DAT was bought in 1931 by Tobata Imono, a large industrial business. Its president, Yoshisuke Ayukawa, had big plans. He wanted to offer a mass-produced Japanese car to compete with American

Below: Datsun had still not made a four-door saloon by the time of this DS model, built in 1949. Its 860cc four-cylinder engine put out 20bhp and drove the rear axle through a three-speed gearbox.

products in the export market.

His wish made a move towards reality with the 1931 DAT prototype small car. And the car started a famous name – it was called Datson; literally the son of DAT.

However, the name was soon changed to Datsun for two reasons. Primarily, it meant that the manufacturers could use the Japanese national emblem of the rising sun. And, since the word 'son' means loss in Japanese, it was totally inappropriate for a product aimed at gaining popularity.

Production started in 1932 and in that year some 150 Datsuns were made in roadster, tourer and saloon versions. With

Right: Station wagon of the early 1950s

a 495cc, four-cylinder engine which developed 10bhp, the top speed was 56km/h (35mph).

The car bore a passing resemblance to the Austin Seven and it has been suggested that it was, indeed, a copy of the Austin. But the similarity ended with appearances because, whereas the Austin used cantilever springs and bevel drive, the Datsun had semi-elliptic rear suspension and worm drive. Quite apart from that, its engine was considerably smaller than that of the British car.

Jidosha Seizo changed its name to Nissan Motor Co. Ltd. at the end of 1933 (the Nissan story is told in detail elsewhere) and production moved from Dsako to new premises at Yokohama. But the name Datsun continued and the thousandth model was built in mid-1934. Exports for that year comprised 44 cars to Spain, India and the United States.

Engine capacity was increased to 725cc in 1935 and it remained that size until after World War II.

Nissan concentrated heavily on commercial vehicles and Datsun cars took second place, a policy typified by the 860cc Thrift of 1951. The engine was used until 1958, albeit in more modern bodywork. The Thrift was replaced with the Austin-based 1.2-litre Bluebird, a name which has survived until today.

Above right: 1972 240C saloon
Below: 1970 240Z works rally car
Bottom: 1974 Cherry coupé

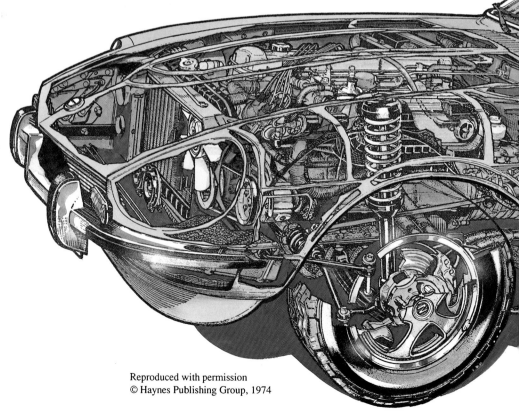

Above: 1974 260Z coupé
Below right: 1974 160B SSS coupé

The Datsun range was growing in complexity in the 1960s with models including the Cedric, President, Fairlady and Skyline. The 240Z sports coupé of 1969 put the company in the performance-car market. It was to become the best-selling sports car in the world with sales exceeding 720,000 by the end of 1980 (including successive models).

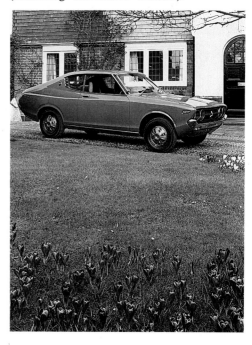

Above: The 1969 240Z was a two-seater coupé powered by a 151bhp six-cylinder engine which drove through a five-speed gearbox. It could reach 201km/h (125mph) and started a famous line of Z-cars.

Left: 1973 120Y estate car

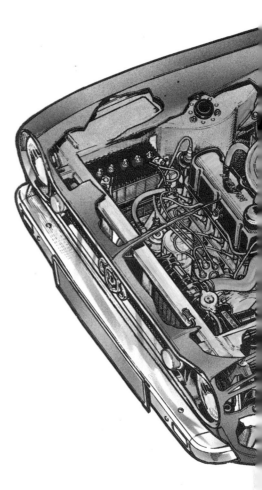

Other popular models included the original rear-wheel-drive Sunny 120Y, the front-wheel-drive Cherry and the Patrol four-wheel-drive Jeep-style vehicle.

The name Datsun was officially dropped at the end of 1983 and thereafter all the company's vehicles have been called Nissans.

Centre: 1979 Violet 160J saloon
Left: 1978 280ZX sports coupé

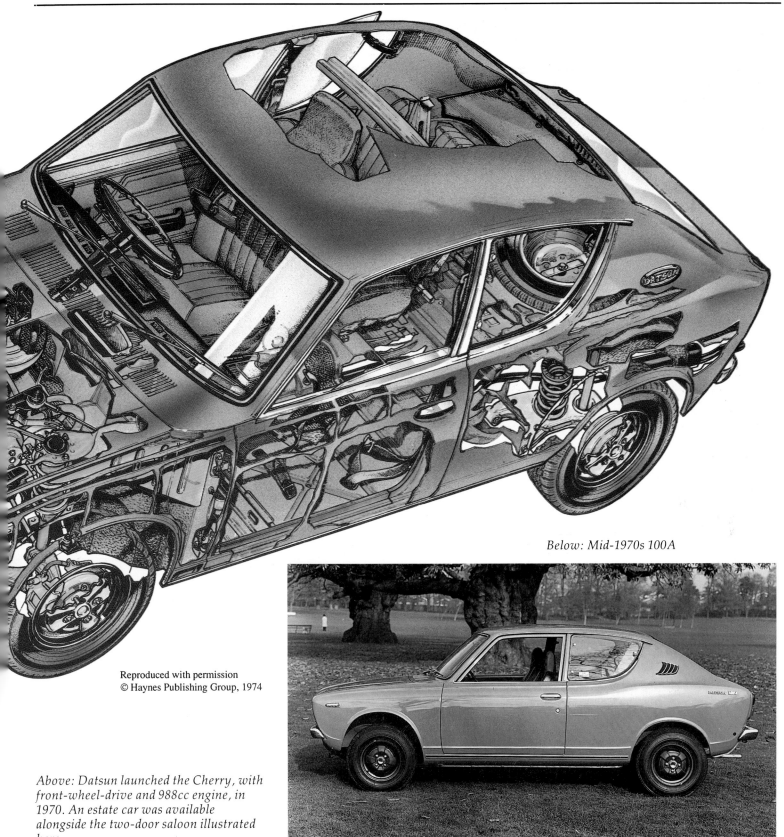

Below: Mid-1970s 100A

Above: Datsun launched the Cherry, with front-wheel-drive and 988cc engine, in 1970. An estate car was available alongside the two-door saloon illustrated here.

De Dietrich
France
1897–1934

The De Dietrich business was originally involved in the manufacture of railway rolling stock – wagons, axles, wheels and carriages. When Alsace and part of Lorraine changed nationality in 1871 the company, now in German territory, set up a new French factory at Lunéville.

One of the families with a controlling interest in the firm was that of Baron Edouard de Türckheim. In 1897 his son,

Above: Lorraine-Dietrich racer, c. 1908

Adrien, acquired a licence to build Amédée Bollée's vehicles at the Lunéville plant. This then became the Société de Dietrich et Cie. de Lunéville, although Bollée cars were also built by De Dietrich in Germany.

After a disappointing performance in the 1901 Paris-Madrid event, De Dietrich progressed to vehicles designed by Léon Turcar and Simon Méry. The German operation built Georges Richard designs and the following year contracted Ettore Bugatti.

In 1904 Adrian de Türckheim left to start up Société Lorraine d'Anciens Etablissements de Dietrich et Cie., with backing from his father, brother and Turcat-Méry. The new vehicles became Lorraine-Dietrichs by 1905, production moving to the modern Argenteuil factory the following year.

In 1907 the company acquired Ariel in England and Isotta-Fraschini of Italy,

Above: 1904 24hp Paris-Madrid racer

without notable effect. Two years later, recession and losses caused it to sell these acquisitions. De Groullard joined the firm around this time, introducing more-modern engines and designing the enormous 15-litre chain-driven Grand Prix racer of 1912.

Marius Barbarou joined Lorraine-Dietrich during World War I and although his initial post-war vehicle, with a sidevalve six-cylinder engine, was unexciting, the later 15CV was more successful. The firm also enjoyed some sporting victories, including two at Le Mans, and under commercial direction from coachbuilder Gaston Grummer, stylish bodywork and slick advertising were introduced. By 1928 the marque became known simply as Lorraine.

The company's interests moved towards aero-engines in the early 1930s, leading to closure of its car department in 1934 – although Tatras were later produced under licence at Argenteuil.

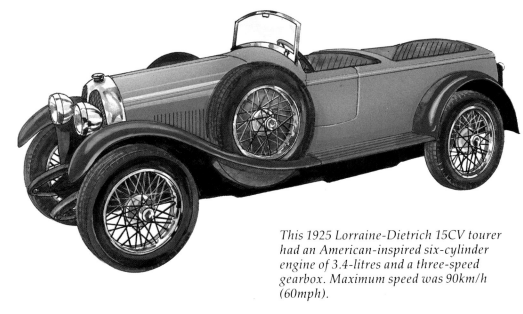

This 1925 Lorraine-Dietrich 15CV tourer had an American-inspired six-cylinder engine of 3.4-litres and a three-speed gearbox. Maximum speed was 90km/h (60mph).

Above: 1907 Lorraine-Dietrich 24/30hp
Below: Late 1920s Lorraine cabriolet

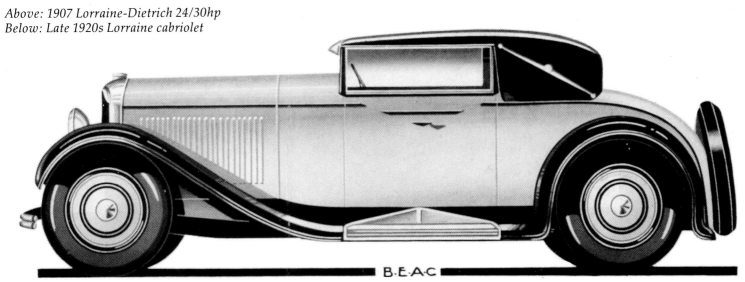

De Dion-Bouton

France
1883–1932

Count Albert de Dion went into partnership with Georges Bouton and his brother-in-law Trépardoux, makers of steam tricycles, in 1883. Although their early vehicles were mainly commercials, they built a car which was to put up the fastest time in the Paris–Rouen Trials of 1894. Trépardoux was so against this experimentation with petrol engines, however, that he resigned from the partnership that year and the De Dion-Bouton name was founded.

Before this Trépardoux had designed the famous De Dion axle system, whereby the vehicle's load-bearing structure and the drive transmission were separated.

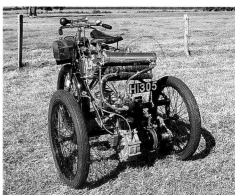

Below: This 1903 De Dion-Bouton Populaire model had its engine at the front and a steering wheel in place of the earlier tiller.

Above left: 1894 petrol tricycle
Top: 1899 single-cylinder model
Above: 1900 tricycle

De Dion lacked finance for large-scale production after World War I, its 1919 range consisting of an in-line four-cylinder engine and two V8s, which were phased out in 1923. A luxury vehicle was introduced the next year, followed by an economy car and a light van in 1926, although this was too late to prevent the firm's closure in 1927.

There followed a brief revival by the French Government until 1932, when car production ceased, although small numbers of commercial vehicles were made until as recently as 1950.

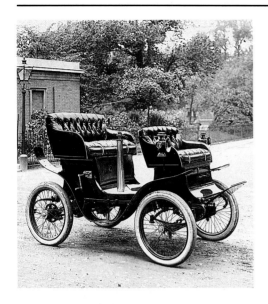

Above: 1902 402cc model
Right: 1908 TT racer
Below centre: 1904 type AD four-cylinder model
Below bottom: 1906 24hp formal town carriage

Bouton developed a high-speed engine capable of 2000rpm – twice the then-accepted norm. Until 1902, these engines were fitted to a variety of De Dion vehicles, initially using frames from Decauville, then Clément.

In 1898 the company received a large injection of cash from Baron van Zuylen and reorganized, selling off various patents. The first voiturette was introduced in 1899, replacing the earlier tricycles. Electric cars were also built, and commercials went into production in 1903, when the company built its first front-engined vehicle.

The company was reorganized a second time in 1908, and also produced bicycles for five years from 1909. De Dion himself, now a Marquis, also branched out unsuccessfully into machine-tool manufacture at St. Ouen.

In 1910 the company introduced a V8 engine, and single-cylinder units disappeared two years later. The company even produced a 14.8-litre-engined prototype which had double rear tyres, but generally speaking, its range was becoming more and more conventional, the commercial vehicles in particular gaining importance.

Right: 1913 50hp V8 model
Below right: 1913 26hp owner-driver saloon

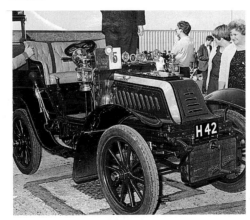

Delage

France
1905–1954

Louis Delage was born in Cognac, France, in 1874. At the age of 31, having previously worked for Turgan-Foy and Peugeot, he set up his own motor-engineering workshop in Levallois, Paris, with Augustine Legros, a former workmate at Peugeot.

Delage had always been interested in racing, and one of his De Dion-engined models finished second in the 1906 Coupe des Voiturettes, following this with a win two years later. Demand for the cars grew and within the next few years Delage began manufacturing his own engines and running gear.

During World War I the company profited greatly from munitions, returning

Above: 1911 12hp 1.4-litre model   *Below: 1919 Type CO six-cylinder*

Above: 1924 D1 Super Sports by Kolsch

Below: In the 1920s, Delage were noted for their fast touring cars, of which this elegant and rakish D1 Super Sports model was typical.

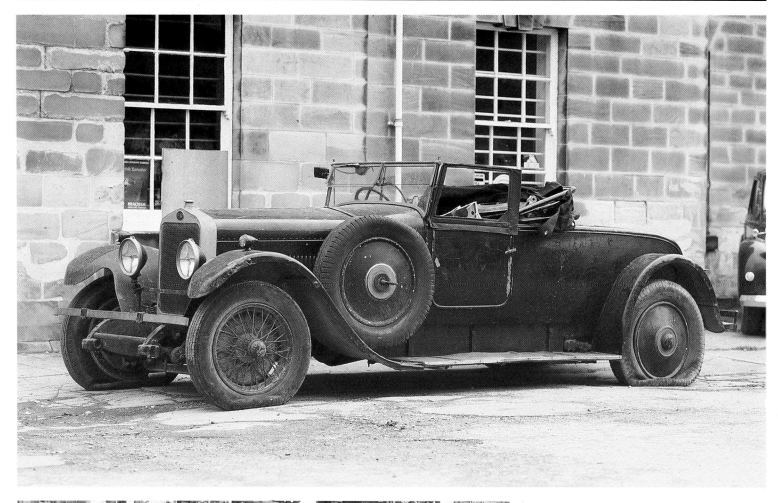

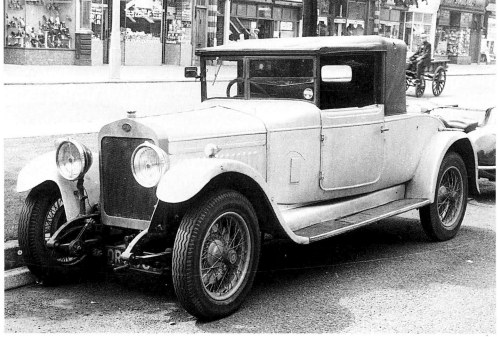

Above: 1927 Albany-bodied DM
Left: 1928 DM 3.2-litre

successfully to cars with the Charles Planchon-designed two-litre DE. A hard-headed man, Delage later sacked Planchon on the spot when his hastily prepared 10.7-litre V12 was forced to retire from the 1923 French Grand Prix.

High living and expensive – though largely victorious – forays into Grand Prix racing brought about Louis Delage's financial downfall. Racing stopped at the end of 1927, although the company did have five major wins to its name.

Some of Delage's finest cars were produced in the late 1920s and early 1930s, but the Depression affected sales and by 1934 the company was floundering. Hasty attempts to introduce smaller-engined cars without sufficient testing gave Delage a bad name. In 1935 all the company's assets were bought by Walter Watney, the Paris

Above: 1930 D8 eight-cylinder

Above: 1935 D6 3-litre cabriolet

Below: 1938 D8 120 sports saloon

Below: From 1932 a super-sports version of the 4-litre D8 was available. Although the car pictured has elegant coachwork, the chassis was often over-bodied. A D8 super-sports took International class records at 180km/h (112mph).

Delage agent, who sold off much of the engineering side, instead making an agreement with Delahaye to build badge-engineered cars to that company's design.

Delage continued in this form until 1953 and, together with Delahaye, merged with Hotchkiss the following year.

Although he remained on the board as a figurehead, Louis Delage lost his money with his company and died poor at the age of 73.

Delahaye

France
1894–1954

Several times during its 60 years of car production, the French firm of Delahaye must have seriously considered changing its name to 'Déja vu' – as anyone attempting to trace the path the company followed would be doomed to going round in several sets of circles.

It commenced making cars in 1894 when a young engineer with experience of locomotive engines, Emile Delahaye, took over a brick-making machinery factory at Tours and successfully changed its direction to car manufacture.

This was just in time for the golden age of town-to-town racing over France's country roads, and two of the first 6hp tubular-framed rear-engined Delahayes were entered for the 1896 Paris–Marseilles–Paris event, finishing sixth and eighth respectively.

In 1898 the firm moved to Paris, and appointed as works manager the man who was to run the company until its eventual demise, Charles Weiffenbach. Emile

Delahaye himself retired in 1901 due to ill health and died four years later, leaving Weiffenbach to continue guiding the company's fortunes.

Above: Luxury for 1900, the 6hp model

He did well, continuing to enter Delahayes in road-races with a modicum of success until 1902 when racing cars grew more specialized and it was deemed too expensive to continue. The new models of that year, though, showed that the firm had gained from its experience; the Type 10B boasted a proper steering wheel, a three-speed gearbox and chain drive. Over 800 were sold, including light-van versions, and this success was followed by

The 1938 Type 135 was one of the classic Delahaye designs; its beautifully-engineered chassis with independent front suspension and its powerful 3.5-litre engine made it popular among coachbuilders.

ever-faster, more sophisticated vehicles – and usually a step up-market from their predecessors. By 1905 the top-of-the-range eight-litre car was good enough for King Alfonso of Spain, a notable connoisseur.

By the outbreak of World War I Delahaye was an undoubted success. Weiffenbach had led the company into other markets including England and Germany, other areas including fire-tender and boat-engine manufacture, and had

introduced along the way several innovative design elements like a V6 engine and pressure-lubricated suspension.

When the war ended, Weiffenbach appeared to have lost the knack of building exciting cars – the models of 1919–1930 were exceptionally average – but had acquired the desire to build an empire instead. He attempted to construct an American-style combine with Berliet (which failed) and to introduce mass-production, and then a little later he linked up with Donnet, Unic, and Chenard-Walcker.

The recession reduced sales, though, and things were looking bleak until 1933, when in a clever move the company went back to its roots in racing and started to produce powerful, lightweight sporting cars. A new young designer, Jean Francois, came up with a series of superb cars, one of which took 18 records in 1934 by averaging 172km/h (107mph) over 48 hours on the Montlhéry racetrack.

This was the beginning of a whole new era for the company. While stripped-down

versions of its cars like the famous Type 135 and 145 were winning races, coachbuilders were using the excellent chassis to produce some of the most sleek and elegant grand touring cars ever. On the way the company took over Delage, another famous name in the grand touring field.

This was definitely Delahaye's golden age, and it lasted until well after World War II – the firm survived the war

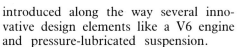

Above: Type 44, advanced for 1911
Right: 1950 235, the essence of French auto style
Below right: Sporting and sleek, the 1938 competition roadster

building lorries, an activity it had never given up, and soon returned to racing and supplying chassis to coachbuilders. On the way the empire-building urge returned, though, and Delahaye swallowed up Simca and several truck-making firms. By the 1950s, though, the market was dwindling for large cars (partly due to French tax laws) so that side of the business suffered badly.

Its last attempt was a Jeep-type vehicle which was, sadly, too complex and sophisticated for the army who eventually settled on the U.S.A.'s simple Jeep, built under licence by Hotchkiss. And as if to add insult to injury, it was Hotchkiss that took over Delahaye in 1954 and stopped car production once and for all. Charles Weiffenbach retired at the point of the takeover and died in 1959.

Above: Classic lines – a 1938 135M

Delaunay-Belleville

France
1904–1950

Formerly a naval engineer, Louis Delaunay joined the well-known marine and locomotive boiler makers, Belleville of St. Denis, Paris, in the 1860s. He moved into a position of power in the company through marriage to the owner's daughter, adding the hyphenated Belleville name to his own in the process.

In 1903 he set up a car factory separate from the firm's other interests, called the Société des Automobiles Delaunay-Belleville, introducing his first model at the Paris Salon of 1904. Three four-cylinder cars appeared that year, designed by Marius Barbarou and Adolphe Clément, with a range of six-cylinder vehicles appearing in 1907.

Until World War I the company's cars, which had no competition history, gained much favour for their air of refined, quiet dignity – and were usually chauffeur-

Above: 1906/7 four-cylinder 20hp model

The firm's advertising of their range of 1910 and thereafter used the phrase 'the car magnificent'. Customers who agreed and bought models like this HB of 1911 included the Tsars of Russia.

driven. Tsar Nicholas II of Russia was a regular customer, as were Trotsky and Lenin after the Revolution. Louis Delaunay-Belleville died in 1912, succeeded by his sons Robert and Pierre, who offered commercial vehicles. Barbarou left to join Lorraine-Dietrich.

During the war Delaunay-Belleville manufactured Hispano-Suiza aero-engines an some heavy military vehicles, in addition to the ships' boilers of the parent company.

After World War I Delaunay continued to produce cars with rounded bonnets and

radiators, although they were now slightly pointed to follow the fashion. The company had lost credence against Hispano-Suiza and Rolls-Royce, however, and this was confirmed when American Continental engines were fitted to the cars from 1931.

Further loss of marque identity came with the 1936 R.16 – very similar to the 230 Mercedes-Benz – which was continued after World War II with an updated 'waterfall' grille.

The last cars and commercials were listed up to 1949/50, but in the initial years

after World War II the Delaunay-Belleville factory concentrated on a 450cc minicar, the Rovin; and the Delauney-Belleville name survives to this day in the shape of a factory making automotive radiators.

Above: A 15hp for the British market

Below: 1910 15hp coachbuilt special

Top: A six-cylinder 26hp model
Above: A 10hp four-cylinder landaulette

De Soto

U.S.A.
1928–1960

The De Soto was a product of the Chrysler Corporation, introduced in 1928 as a medium-priced marque to fill the gap between Plymouth and the mid-priced Dodge. The first models followed the design and styling of contemporary Chryslers and were very successful, but the marque suffered badly during the Depression and never really received the recognition which some of its models deserved. Straight-eight engines were offered in the early years, but the models of the later 1930s and 1940s had six-cylinder engines.

In 1952, an oversquare overhead-valve V8 engine arrived, based on the previous year's hemi-head Chrysler. At the same time, De Soto moved into a new market niche just above Dodge and below Chrysler itself. The last sidevalve straight-six was made in 1954, and only V8s were available in the restyled 1955 models. The less-powerful engine was known as the Firedome, and the more-powerful unit was called the Fireflite. A limited-production high-performance Adventurer hard-top

Above: 1928 Series K model

Right: 1934 Airflow saloon

Below: The 1934 De Soto Airflow was one of several similar Airflow models from Chrysler. Its body/chassis unit foreshadowed full unitary structures but the public could not live with its futuristic shape.

model arrived for 1956, and in 1957 De Soto gained Virgil Exner's new 'Forward-Look' styling, along with other Chrysler products.

Less-powerful but less-expensive V8 engines were standard on the 1958 models, but De Soto was caught by a slump in the sales of medium-priced cars and in 1959 the division was merged with Plymouth.

Above: 1961 Styline hardtop coupé

Below: 1952 Firedome 8, model S-17

Along with other Chrysler products (Imperial excepted), De Soto switched to unitary body construction for 1960, but poor sales resulted in the range being cut back drastically for the 1961 model year and, in fact, only a few examples had been made when De Soto production was axed altogether in November 1960.

De Tomaso

Italy
1956 to date

Alejandro de Tomaso had an unlikely background for a man who was to produce exotic sports cars.

He was born in Buenos Aires in 1928, the son of a former Prime Minister of Argentina who died when Alejandro was five.

Despite later being expected to manage the family's extensive estate he took up motor racing and fled to Italy in 1955 following political pressure.

He met the Maserati brothers and drove their OSCA cars and married American Elizabeth Haskell, herself a racing driver with a family fortune from automotive finance.

He founded De Tomaso Automobili SpA. in Modena, Italy, in 1959 and built his first racing cars around OSCA engines.

His first road-going car, the Ford-engined Vallelunga, sold just over 50 between 1963 and 1965.

An approach to American race tuner Carroll Shelby for Ford engines led to the Mangusta of 1969.

De Tomaso's wife was related to the chairman and president of Rowan Industries, of New Jersey. He persuaded them to take over coachbuilder Ghia and, as a result, he became president of that company in 1967.

Rowan Industries' investment into De Tomaso's car operations allowed room for expansion and the Mangusta was exported to America.

Sales rose to nearly £1 million in 1968, but launching the Mangusta had proved an expensive business and profits slumped.

De Tomaso's next car was the Pantera, aimed at linking Ford with the European performance market. The car was later joined by the Longchamp and Deauville.

De Tomaso had a varied career and in the 1970s bought control of Maserati from Peugeot, bought managing control of Innocenti Mini production and had interests in both boatbuilding and hotels.

The current model is the Pantera GT5-S, capable of 257km/h (160mph).

Top: The classic Ghia lines of the 1966 Mangusta
Above: The epitome of Italian style, the 1966 Pampero

The Pantera was launched in 1970 with a 5.6-litre Ford engine giving it a top speed of 257km/h (160mph). It was luxuriously equipped, with air-conditioning as standard and leather seats.

Above and below: The De Tomaso Guara, first shown in 1993, uses a mid-mounted BMW 4.0-litre V8 engine and a six-speed gearbox

Detroit Electric

U.S.A.
1907–1938

The Detroit Electric Car originated from the well-established firm of carriage builders, the Anderson Carriage Co. Its range of High School horse-drawn surreys, buggies, wagons and carriages had sold at the rate of up to 15,000 a year until the increasing prevalence of motorized vehicles had caused it to look in a new direction.

Anderson's Detroit factory was re-equipped in 1907 for the production of an electrically powered car with no trunk or hood, but rounded battery covers at both ends, which quickly became the most fashionable method of town transport.

Above: 1912-13 Electric brougham built under licence

Below: The 1909 brougham was popular with lady drivers

About this time the company bought the American branch of the British electric-motor manufacturers, Ewell-Parker, and a small number of cars were built by the Scottish Arrol-Johnston firm. The Anderson factory was, by this time, reputed to be the largest producer of such vehicles in the world. Up to World War I in excess of 1,000 cars a year were built there, although after the end of hostilities this number gradually declined.

Anderson was reorganized as the Detroit Electric Car Co. in 1919, having previously become the Anderson Electric Car Co. in 1911. Electric-powered commercial vehicles were also introduced in that year and an attempt was made to update the styling in the early 1920s, with the introduction of false hoods and radiator grilles.

By 1927 Detroit's commercial-vehicle range had been deleted and production was dwindling, being confined to specials made to order using either the pre-World War I horseless carriage styling, or more acceptable coachwork supplied by Willys-Overland.

Jamieson Handy took over the Detroit company in the mid-1930s, and after that time only a handful of the cars were produced, with orders being refused by 1938 when the firm finally closed.

D.K.W.

Germany
1928–1966

Danish-born J. S. Rasmussen started a workshop in Zschopau – now known as Karl-Marx Stadt in East Germany – in 1907, making boiler and heater fittings.

Fellow Dane Mathiessen joined him and they experimented with steam cars. They were called Dampf-Kraft Wagen – the initials of which gave birth to D.K.W.

In 1922, Rasmussen – who by now manufactured light cars and taxis – formed Metallwerke Frankenberg to make components for D.K.W.'s expanding range of motor-cycles. These were commonly known as *Das Kleine Wunder*, which means 'The Little Wonder'.

By 1927, D.K.W. was the world's largest manufacturer of motor-cycles with 40,000 produced in 1928 alone.

Rasmussen's motor company was called Zschopauer Moteren-Werke J. S. Rasmussen A.G. and it produced its first D.K.W. car in 1928. It had a two-stroke twin-cylinder engine and wooden chassis-less construction.

The company had many other interests including the manufacture of components for Audi.

D.K.W.'s first front-wheel-drive cars were the F1 and F2 which came from Audi's design department. Their transmission was soon used by other firms, including Audi and Tornax.

D.K.W. also made large V4-engined cars in Berlin-Spandau at the D-Wagen factory, and smaller cars at Zwickau, the Audi plant. The Zoschopau factory concentrated on engines and motor-cycles.

D.K.W. also built some rear-wheel-drive cars and commercials, including the F8 of 1939.

In 1934, D.K.W. commanded about 15 per cent of the German car market – second only to Opel – when Rasmussen retired.

From 1934 to 1939, D.K.W.s were made in Switzerland as Holka-D.K.W.s and immediately after the war in Sweden at Philipsson-D.K.W.s.

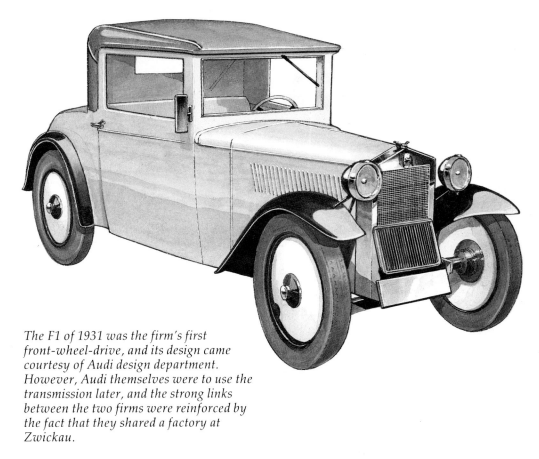

The F1 of 1931 was the firm's first front-wheel-drive, and its design came courtesy of Audi design department. However, Audi themselves were to use the transmission later, and the strong links between the two firms were reinforced by the fact that they shared a factory at Zwickau.

Below: The F1 front-wheel-drive roadster of 1930 boasted 15 horsepower

Some D.K.W.s appeared in East Germany in 1948 from the former Audi factory, and two years later they were joined by versions based on a pre-war three-cylinder F9 prototype. They were known as IFAs and production ended in 1956.

Variants of the two-cylinder Meisterklasse were followed by the F9, and two-stroke cars continued to be made until the end of D.K.W. production in 1966.

Thereafter, the company made only motorcycles and the machines mainly carry the name Hercules, although D.K.W. continues to be used in some export countries.

Above left: A 1937 model proves its strength
Left: The 1938 Reichsklasse, familiar from WWII newsreels

Top: The Berlin-built V4 of 1930
Above: 1953's two-stroke Auto Union/DKW
Below: The very American DKW 1000 of 1959

Doble

U.S.A.
1914–1931

Abner Doble, born in San Francisco in 1895, built his steam-powered car when he was only 16. His later products were considered the finest in the world, particularly in America, where the use of steam for passenger-carrying vehicles was to persist longer than anywhere else.

After studying at the Massachusetts Institute of Technology where he built what became the Model A, Doble set up his own company. The Abner Doble Motor Vehicle Co., of Waltham, Massachusetts, started in 1914, with financial backing from his parents.

Here, Doble made five model As, selling four and keeping the last for development into the Model B and C – for which he needed more money. This came from Detroit, Doble joining up with C. L. Lewis, latterly of the Consolidated Car Co., to become the General Engineering Co. by 1916.

The new vehicle, the GEC Doble, or Doble-Detroit, was due to be launched the following year, reputedly with 11,000 advance orders. Unfortunately, the war priorities of the American government would not allow Doble and Lewis the quantities of steel they required for large-scale production and the project had faded by 1918.

After the war, Doble moved west to California, setting up a new factory as the Doble Steam Motors Corporation in Emeryville, planning to restart production in 1924.

His new car was the Model E, which he showed to the public at the San Francisco Auto Show in 1923. This was a highly sophisticated car, without many of the drawbacks commonly associated with steam-powered vehicles, such as slow starting from cold. It was available with a variety of luxurious and elegant body styles made by Walter Murphy of Pasadena. Plans were for 300 cars a year to begin with, later rising to 1,000 a year.

Shortly after this Doble was extensively

Above: The luxurious Phaeton of 1923   *Below: The De Luxe Runabout version*

Right: Front view of the impressive chassis

swindled on the stock market, and faced massive debts. The Emeryville factory and land set aside for new development were either mortgaged or sold, with only a limited number of Model Es and the new F being produced. Planned production of the Doble-Simplex economy car also collapsed.

In 1931 the company went bankrupt. Doble himself worked on steam-powered commercials in Germany and on the 1950 Paxton Phoenix and the 1956 Keen, neither of which was successful.

Dodge

U.S.A.
1914 to date

The Dodge brothers, John and Horace, began as bicycle manufacturers, progressing to engine producers for Ford and becoming shareholders in that company as a result. The brothers began developing their own car in 1911, which finally came out in 1914.

The Dodge 4s were tough vehicles favoured as staff cars and ambulances during World War I. In 1915, when 45,000 were made, the company ranked third in the production stakes, rising to second behind Ford in 1920.

Left: 1915 Dodge, known for its toughness   Above: The first Dodge automobile, 1914

Above: The 1924 touring model

Above: 1928 'Victory 6' sedan   Below: Victory 6, with hydraulic brakes

In that year both brothers died, and Fred J. Haynes became president. The Graham truck business began using Dodge components in large numbers. Five years later Dodge was sold to the Dillon Read & Co. firm of bankers, passing to Chrysler in 1928, with K. T. Keller replacing Haynes. At this time sales had been slipping due to competition from Chrysler marques,

Above: The 1925 model, beginning to date
Below: The 1929 Dodge 8

The Polara Lancer of 1960 was typical of the huge, tailfinned, heavily chrome-laden monsters of the late '50s and early '60s. It had a V8 5916cc engine and a three-speed automatic gearbox.

Top: 1954 Dodge V8
Centre: 1957 Dodge Royal
Above left: 1940s D-14 De Luxe
Above: 1959 Custom Royal

although 1927 saw Dodge commercials being assembled at Kew, Surrey, in Britain.

The Ram mascot appeared in 1931 and sales improved after the Depression, but during the 1940s Dodges became almost indistinguishable from De Sotos and luxury Plymouths.

Dodge heavy military vehicles were successful during World War II, commercial production taking place from Warren, Detroit, while the cars were still made at Hamtramck, Detroit.

The new Red Ram V8 engine appeared in 1953, and Dodge have since offered more sporting saloons, such as the Charger coupé of 1966, as well as compacts.

At the end of the 1960s came the remarkable Daytona Charger, now considered a classic; and into the early 1970s the semi-compact Dart, medium-sized Coronet and larger Polara were offered. A range of sports pickups was introduced at this time and Mitsubishi sub-compacts were also available.

Above: The 1972 Monaco　　　*Below: The modern Shadow ES*

Above: Today's Dodge Colt GT
Below: The Dodge Omni

Renault took over the European commercial-vehicle side in the early 1980s, while the car side is allied closely to the Plymouth range. The startling V10 Viper concept car was displayed during 1988, with talk of production in 1990.

Right: The Dodge Grand Caravan with new 3.3-litre V6 engine

Above: 1990 Spirit LE

Below: The Daytona Shelby

Below: 1990 streamlined Daytona ES

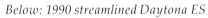

Below: The Daytona was developed from the Chrysler K-car, a well-balanced saloon with front-wheel-drive. From the early days with just the ordinary 2.2-litre ohc four, it was developed with turbo-charging and intercooling to produce 174bhp.

The launch of the outrageous Viper in 1992 really put the Dodge badge back on the map. With a snarling, 400bhp, 8.0-litre V10 engine and massive chrome pipes, the open-topped 2-seater supercar started a bidding war among keen early customers, with some willing to cough up as much as three times the $50,000 asking price. Although it was a nineties sports car, it was distinctly low-tech compared to the competition: but this seemed to be what buyers wanted – a raw and exciting road racer. It became an instant legend and was often described as a modern-day Cobra. The V10 engine wasn't just used in the Viper, and appeared again in a monstrous and powerful pick-up, named the Dodge Ram.

Otherwise, the new-look Dodge range echoed that of Chrysler and Plymouth but with trim levels suitably adjusted to suit the targeted Dodge buyer. Although, in fact, on some markets, the Viper was Chrysler-badged.

Above right: The Dodge Viper RT/10 Roadster with 8.0-litre V10

Below: The Dodge Neon R/T

Above: Dodge Stratus

Left: 1998 Dodge Avenger

Below: Dodge Caravan

Above: 1998 Dodge Intrepid

Below Dodge Viper GTS Coupé

Duesenberg

U.S.A.
1920–1937

Fred Duesenberg began making bicycles before going on to design his famous horizontal overhead-valve engine for the Mason car. Together with his brother August he set up independently to build racing and marine engines under a variety of names.

In 1916 the Duesenberg Motors Corporation was formed in connection with J. R. Harbeck, managing director of Loew-Victor, although the Duesenberg brothers themselves put no money into the venture. A new factory was built at Elizabeth in New Jersey, in which Bugatti-designed aero-engines were manufactured during World War I.

After the war the brothers left the Duesenberg Motors Corporation and the rights to Fred's horizontal-valve engine were sold to Rochester Motors who, in turn, sold engines of that design to various luxury-car manufacturers. Instead, the brothers decided to launch a car of their own, which they did in 1920 with the Model A, having formed Duesenberg Automobile and Motors Co. Inc. in the March of that year.

Indianapolis was an important event for the Duesenberg company, because their racers (above and below) often won the event, providing both valuable publicity and engine development.

Below: The Model A, like this 1922 example, was a sound enough car for its day, but poor management and production problems led to the receivers being called in.

Above: 1925 Model A eight-cylinder roadster
Left: 1930 Duesenberg Model J roadster

Poor management led to the receivers being called in by 1924, but the following year the Ducsenberg Motor Co. appeared, with new finance and Fred as President. By this time the Model A was no longer so innovative and the negligibly changed Model X brought out at that time did little to revive the newer company's flagging fortunes. In 1926, however, Errett Lobban Cord, controller of Auburn Automobiles, gained control of the company with the idea of adding Duesenberg's still-successful competition name to a new prestige car.

As Duesenberg Inc. the brothers were given the brief to build an entirely new car, which came out in 1928. Called the Model J, it was the most remarkable car of its day, being very fast and of advanced design. The Duesenberg-designed engines

Above: The prestigious 1932 Model J

The Model J, announced in 1928, was financed by the Cord company, and thanks to their development cash it proved to be one of the greatest cars built in the U.S.A. Its enormous engine had more than twice the power of any other American car.

were built by another company owned by Cord, Lycoming. The Model J could be bought either fully coach-built or as a chassis to take bodywork of the owner's choice. The company preferred to sell complete cars, with bodies of its own design but made by recommended builders such as Murphy, Le Baron, Derham, Bohman & Schwartz and Judkins. Model Js were owned by Al Jolson and Clark Gable.

By 1932 a supercharged version, the Model SJ, was produced. Only 36 of this model were made, but many of the earlier J cars were subsequently supercharged or merely fitted with the instantly recognizable external chrome exhausts to look like the SJ. Unfortunately, although Duesenberg survived the Depression, the Cord Corporation did not, and the final collapse of this organization in 1937 also took Duesenberg with it. The Cord-owned companies were sold off and the Duesenberg factory was turned over to Marmon-Herrington for the production of trucks until the mid-1950s.

In 1947 Augie Duesenberg was involved in an attempt to revive the famous marque but nothing ever came of it. Fred had died in a car crash in 1932 and by 1955 Augie, too, was dead.

Further attempts were made by members of the Duesenberg family to revive the marque. In 1966 Augie's son Fritz brought out a prototype for a Chrysler-powered sedan, designed by Virgil Exner and built by Ghia in Italy. In 1979 Fred's sons Harlan and Kenneth and Augie's brother Wesley tried again, this time with a limousine based on a Cadillac. Both were unsuccessful, with only one prototype car being built in each case.

It is fair to say that the marque died then, although between 1971 and 1979 the California-based Duesenberg Motor Co. (without family connection) produced around 12 replicas of the SSJ roadster. Other attempts by various outsiders have been made since to copy the famous and distinctive Duesenberg design of the 1920s.

Above right: 1931 6.9-litre, eight-cylinder Model J
Centre right: 1933 Model SJ speedster with distinctive exhaust pipes
Right: 1936 Model SJN convertible coupé

Index